A Summer Affair

Jenness Jordan

PublishAmerica
Baltimore

© 2005 by Jenness Jordan.
All rights reserved. No part of this book may be reproduced, stored in a retrieval system or transmitted in any form or by any means without the prior written permission of the publishers, except by a reviewer who may quote brief passages in a review to be printed in a newspaper, magazine or journal.

First printing

ISBN: 1-4137-6821-0
PUBLISHED BY PUBLISHAMERICA, LLLP
www.publishamerica.com
Baltimore

Printed in the United States of America

Dedication:

This book is dedicated to my three girls, Ariana, Cassie, and Vikki.

They have been my motivation to keep pursuing my dream and to never want to settle for anything less.

Girls, Dreams Do Come True!

Acknowledgments:

Primarily, I need to give thanks to God for the gift of creativity and love of writing that he has given me. Next, I want to thank my three beautiful daughters for their patience, love, and individuality. Having them in my life gives me a reason to keep moving forward. To Donna Vigeant, Eric Lyons, Heidi Draughn, and Laura Macdonald, thank you for always being there for me. You never ran away when the pressure was on. Thank you for all of your unique qualities that I love so much. I would also like to thank Eric Lyons for showing me how to love unselfishly.

I would also like to give thanks to adult contemporary singer Michael Bolton for his inspirational voice, music, and humanitarian acts, which have helped me through some tough times in my life. Mr. Bolton and my friend Eric are truly two of the few angels/heroes that we have left in the world.

For Amanda, Brianne, Malhana, Kim, Erin, and Heidi - thanks for your support. To the best heavy metal band on earth, KISS- you will always be #1 and thank you for being in the world. I still love you. Finally, for those who read this book- This is the 1st installment of the series and there is a bit of truth in each story.

Table of Contents

7	Chapter 1	The Meeting
25	Chapter 2	It's a Long Day
43	Chapter 3	The Concert
64	Chapter 4	Humiliation
77	Chapter 5	The Accident
99	Chapter 6	The Surprise
110	Chapter 7	Rhode Island
120	Chapter 8	Runaway
134	Chapter 9	Choices/Farewell

− 1 −
The Meeting

It was about four o'clock when we arrived at the bus station in Portland. My brother and I picked up our carry-on bags, got off the bus, and went to go find our grandmother who was supposed to meet us there. She was waiting outside the terminal in a lavender sun dress with a smile and open arms. The bus driver handed our luggage to us from the undercarriage compartment. Then we walked over to Grammy's Cadillac and put them in the trunk. We agreed to grab a bite to eat before heading back on the road. We looked around and found a little family restaurant across from the bus station.

We crossed the busy intersection when it was safe and then headed into the restaurant. It was a quaint and cozy little place. On all of the tables were baskets filled with a variety of flowers. Various pictures of mountains, gardens, and countryside cottages hung nicely in between each window. The aroma that came from the kitchen reminded me of my mother's cooking. After we ate our tuna, bacon, and lettuce sandwiches, Grammy paid the tab and left a tip for the server so that we could be on our way.

As soon as we got to Grammy's house, I noticed it was the same as it when I was last there five years earlier. I retrieved my luggage, brought it into the house and upstairs to my old room. My room also hadn't changed; it was just the way I had left it: messy! Feeling a little childish, I hopped on the bed and began jumping on it as I used to. When I was done being a child, I unpacked my stuff then went downstairs for some entertainment. I relaxed in the den watching TV for a little while and then took a nice hot bath to relax. Afterwards I put on my nightgown, went upstairs to my room, said my prayers, and went to bed.

The next morning I awoke to the sun on my face that was lighting up the whole room. After breakfast was over, we cleaned up the kitchen and headed to the lake. Grammy told us that she would be back to pick us up around five o'clock. I walked over to the ladies room to change into my bathing suit and then joined my brother.

As I laid the blanket out across the sand, I turned to him and asked, "Are you going swimming?"

"Yes. What about you?" he replied.

"I think I'm going to lie out for a while and catch some rays," I told him.

A few minutes later, my brother walked over to the dock while I put my suntan lotion on. I decided to work on the front part of my body first, so I lay down on my back. All of a sudden I felt some dirt or sand fall on me so I looked up to see where it had come from. I lifted my hand into the blinding light and saw a guy with shoulder-length blond hair standing over me. He wore a red and blue bandana around his head, a black t-shirt, and blue jeans that were worn and ripped. His eyes were like a clear blue ocean and they lit up when he smiled.

"I'm sorry. Did I get you?" he asked.

"Yes, but it was only a little bit," I replied.

"You don't remember me, do you?" he questioned.

"No. I'm sorry, I don't," I told him.

"I'm Warren, Warren Charles from down the street," he smiled.

"Didn't we go to school together or something?"

"Yes, junior high, about six or seven years ago."

"Oh yeah, now I remember. You used to pull my pony tail when we rode the bus," I chuckled.

"If I remember correctly, I wasn't the only one. I believe that your brother had a hand in it, as well," he laughed and then went on to ask, "By the way, where is that little twerp, anyway?"

"He's over on the dock," I said, pointing towards the water.

"Well, I'm going to go over and say hi. Maybe we can all get together later," Warren said as he walked towards the shoreline.

As the day went on, I met more people, mainly girls, and even went swimming for a little while. A few of the girls and I just sat around the blanket talking and listening to the radio. Then I saw this guy with long brown hair and a dark tan walk over to the picnic table where Warren, my brother, and some other guys were sitting. He was so gorgeous! I couldn't take my eyes off him.

I turned to the girl next to me and asked, "Who is that guy with the nice tan over there talking to Warren?"

"Do you mean the one that just walked over there?" she questioned with a grin.

"Yes," I replied.

"That's Mitch Lafferty. He's a big-time player," she answered.

"What do you mean?"

"He sleeps around even if he has a girlfriend, which he does," she replied.

"Bummer. He looks like such a nice guy. What a waste!" I sighed.

"If you want, I can still introduce you to him and some of the other guys," she suggested as she pointed to some of the other possibilities in the group.

We walked over to the picnic table and sat down. I was so nervous that I could feel the sweat forming on my palms and the butterflies in my stomach.

"Everyone, I would like for you to meet Victoria. Victoria, this is Mitch Lafferty, Daniel Goff, Brian Schultz, Chris Brown, James Price, and Vince Tucker," she said while trying to catch her breath.

"Hi, it's nice to meet you all," I said with a smile, and went on to say, "I think you forgot someone."

"I don't think I did. Who could I have forgotten?" she replied, looking a little puzzled.

"The person that you forgot is a girl, and that girl is you," I said pointing my finger at her.

"Oh. Silly me! Hi, my name is Katrina, and you must be Matthew's sister, Victoria," she chuckled as she extended her hand out to me for a friendly handshake.

"Would you ladies like to come to the party later?" Chris asked us.

"Sure, I'd love to," Katrina replied.

"I don't think that my brother and I will be able to," I told him.

"Why not?" Katrina sadly asked.

"My grandmother is coming to get us and I doubt that she will want us going to a party," I replied.

"Aren't you over eighteen?" Warren asked me.

"Yes, but Matthew isn't. My grandmother is very set in her ways," I explained.

"Well, you don't have to tell her that you're going to a party. You can just say that you're spending the night at Katrina's house," Chris smiled as he gave me a wink.

"I don't really like to lie," I said.

"You wouldn't be if you really did spend the night at her house. Then you would be able to go to the party," Daniel said.

"That might work, but what about Matthew?" I replied.

"He can spend the night at my house," Warren answered.

"Okay, I guess that I can try and talk my grandmother into it," I told everyone.

When my grandmother arrived, my brother and I walked over to the car to ask about spending the night. After a few minutes of begging, she finally said yes. She told us that she would bring our overnight stuff to our friends' houses and then pick us up in the morning. As she drove off, we walked back over to the table where everyone was waiting.

"So, don't keep us in suspense, tell us what happened," Katrina asked, drumming her fingers on the table.

"She said yes," I told her.

"Wow, that's great! Now we can get down to business," Chris smiled, looking right at me.

"Right on, how about the girls supply the food and the guys can bring the alcohol?" James suggested.

"You can't have a party without music?" Katrina asked.

"I'll take care of the music," Mitch answered.

We all went in different directions and did the jobs that we were supposed to do. While Katrina and I were in the store getting food, we began discussing what we were going to do at the party.

"I think I'm just going to sit around, listen to some music, and maybe eat a little bit," I said.

"Not me. I'm going to do a little dancing and maybe even ask Warren to dance," she smiled.

"Do you like Warren?" I asked her.

"Yes, but I'm not ready for a serious relationship yet," she answered as she picked up some chips and dip.

"Just be careful, there are a lot of diseases out in the world nowadays," I told her.

"I'm not going to sleep around," she replied loudly as we got up to the register.

"Keep it down, everyone is looking at us," I whispered to her as I looked around at the people staring at us.

"Sorry," she whispered back, looking down at her feet.

"What are you going to wear?" Katrina asked as we got into her '87 Camaro.

"What I have on," I answered.

"We can go to my house and change if you want," she suggested.

"No, that's okay; I'll stick to my jean shorts and t-shirt," I replied.

When we got back to the beach, we put everything on the picnic table and walked over to a little wooden bridge where everybody was waiting.

"Glad to see that you ladies finally decided to show up," Mitch chuckled.

"The lines in the store were long," I told him.

"Enough talking, let's get this party going," Brian said, walking towards the table.

"Hey Vicki, I think Chris likes you," Katrina whispered as we were walking.

"What makes you think that?" I asked her.

"Because he hasn't taken his eyes off of you since we got back," she answered.

"No way, you're just reading too much into it," I told her.

"You'll see," she replied picking up a plate off the table.

As I began putting some food on my plate, I felt someone's hand brush mine. I looked up and saw Chris standing there.

"I'm sorry; I didn't mean to scare you," he smiled as he backed up a little.

"That's okay," I replied.

"I was wondering if you wouldn't mind sitting with me while we eat," he suggested.

"Sure, I guess so," I told him.

We walked over to the dock and sat down at the end. As I started to eat, I felt Chris putting his arm around my waist. His hand went slowly up the side of my waist towards my chest. I wanted to pull away, but the sensation from his caress kept me close.

"I promise I won't do anything that you don't want me to do," he whispered softly in my ear.

"I want to but—" I started to say but hesitated.

"But what?" he asked.

"It's just, this really isn't the time or the place, and we

barely know each other," I answered as I stood up with my back to him.

"I'm sorry if you took what I did the wrong way," he started to say as he stood up next to me, then went on to say, "I wasn't expecting to have sex with you. I just wanted to touch and maybe even kiss you."

"Then I guess it's me who should apologize, not you," I said.

He gently grabbed my arm, turned me towards him then said, "You have nothing to be sorry for. I'm the one who made the advances."

"Well, I'll accept your apology if you accept mine," I said politely.

"Okay, but on one condition," he replied.

"What's that?" I asked.

"If you would do me the honor and have one dance with me," Chris answered.

"Sure, I'd love to," I smiled.

"Great! Let's go over to the table where everybody else is," he exclaimed, taking my hand and leading me over to the spot.

"Wait! What about our food?" I asked as I tried to catch my breath while we were running.

"Don't worry; it will still be there when we get back. If not, I'll get you some more," he replied as we approached the table.

Chris pulled me close to him with his arms wrapped tightly around me. I put my arms around his neck and laid my head on his firm but soft chest. I closed my eyes so that I could relax and enjoy the moment. The night seemed so peaceful and full of music with all of nature's life talking and mingling with the soft sounds coming from the radio. It was almost like a dream. His hand brushed across the side of my face, pushing back my long auburn hair, and then he gently kissed my forehead. He moved his hand under my chin and slowly lifted my head to meet with his. We stared hopelessly into each others eyes as if we knew what the other was thinking. Then it happened! Our lips touched in a soft but firm kiss, which caused sparks to ignite throughout my whole body.

Just as we were getting deeper into the kiss, I heard footsteps from behind me getting closer. I hoped that whoever it was wouldn't interrupt us. Of course, they did.

"I don't mean to disturb you two love birds, but I was wondering if I could cut in for just one moment," a familiar voice from behind said.

"If it's all right with the lady and you don't take too long," Chris hinted.

"I guess its okay," I said shrugging my shoulders.

"I promise that it will only be a few minutes," Mitch said as he stepped in front of me and took my hand.

"I'll be back in a few minutes and we'll finish up where we left off," Chris told me as he kissed my lips then turned and walked away.

"So, what did you want or am I assuming too much?" I asked Mitch.

"No, you're right. I wanted to see if you would meet me later so we could talk," he answered.

"What do we need to talk about?" I inquired.

"I'll explain later, just meet me on the side of the library in about half an hour," he replied.

"I don't know. Chris will probably want to spend the night with me," I told him.

"It'll be just for a few minutes, please," he pleaded quietly.

"I'll talk to him about it and let you know," I said.

"No, don't say anything to him. Just tell him that you're going to the store for a few things," he suggested.

"And what if I don't come back anything? He'll get suspicious."

"Let me worry about that, okay?"

"Well, let me think about it." I pulled away and walked over to the table where Chris was.

While we were all sitting around, Brian decided to start a fire so that we could toast marshmallows. Chris picked up a stick, stuck two marshmallows on it, and then began cooking them. I sat in between his legs so that I could lie down comfortably and maybe he would think that I wanted him to feed them to me. A few minutes later the marshmallows were golden brown. Then he fed them to me.

A couple of hours later everybody began packing up and leaving. I looked around for Katrina and spotted her walking over to the wooden bridge with Mitch. They seemed to be talking about some serious stuff, because I noticed Mitch's arms flying around as if he was frustrated. Minutes later I saw Mitch walk away and Katrina walk towards me. She motioned me to meet her over by the restroom. I told Chris where I was going and went to meet her.

"Mitch really wants to talk to you. He said it was important," she said as I walked into the room.

"Do you know what about?" I asked her.

"I think that it has something to do with Chris," Katrina answered.

"What about him?" I questioned.

"He really didn't want me to tell you, but I guess that I can fill you in on a little of it so you'll know what to expect when you talk to him," she replied.

"Okay, I'm ready," I told her as I lit up a cigarette.

"Basically, he's going to warn you about Chris," she said.

"Warn me! Warn me about what?" I exclaimed.

"I guess he's bad news or something, I don't know. That's why you need to talk to Mitch," she replied.

"Fine, I'll talk to him with Chris there, because I don't think that it's fair to talk about people without them there to defend themselves," I told her.

"I understand what you're saying, but I think that will cause a fight between them. So, maybe you could just give Mitch a chance to tell you what he knows," Katrina explained.

"Give who a chance to say what?" a voice called out from the dark.

Katrina said as I turned and saw Chris standing behind me.

"Hi, I was just on my way to find you," I said to Chris, giving him a friendly kiss on the cheek.

"Don't try and squirm your way out," he said as he grabbed my arm and held me against the wall.

"Chris, please let go. You're hurting me," I cried.

"Not until you give me a straight answer," he said.

"Let her go!" Katrina shouted.

"I will once she tells me what I want to know," he growled as his angry eyes stared down into my fearful eyes.

"Okay, it's not a big deal. I was just telling her that she should give you a chance to ask her about you two dating," Katrina explained, then went on to say, "Now, I don't know if she should even bother."

"What are you talking about?" he asked as he let me go.

"What I mean is that she wanted to ask you out but was afraid that you would think that she was too aggressive. But, like I said before, I don't think that she should bother after this little episode," Katrina explained as she took me by the hand and led me outside. "I cannot believe the nerve of that guy. Who the heck does he think he is, behaving like that?"

"I know I always pick some real winners," I sighed.

"Don't be so down on yourself. You didn't know he would react like that. Maybe that's what Mitch wanted to tell you about later," Katrina replied, patting my back as we approached the table.

I think that I'll head up to your house now, if you don't mind," I said.

"No, I don't mind. I'll even go with you," she suggested.

"You don't have to; I don't want to ruin your night," I told her.

"Don't be silly!" she exclaimed.

"I'm not. I just want you to have some fun with your friends and maybe even with a nice guy," I replied.

"I can still have fun with my friends tonight," Katrina said.
"What do you mean?" I asked her.
"I'll invite a few people up to the house for a little while."
"What if Chris tries to come along?"
"Not to worry, I'll fill the guys in and they'll make sure that he doesn't. Wait here for a minute and I'll be right back with the guys. Then we can head to my house," she said as she walked over to the dock.

A chill came over me and my whole body quivered, so I went over to the fire to get warm. I think that part of the reason for the chill was the night air by the water; the other part was because I was a little freaked out about the way Chris had acted. He seemed so nice, but I guess everyone behaves differently after they've had a few drinks. *That is still no excuse to man handle someone though, especially when you don't have a good reason or even know the person,* I thought to myself as I started back over to the table. Just then, I noticed Chris walking my way so I turned around and headed towards the dock. I could hear his voice calling out to me, but I kept going as if I didn't. My heart was pounding and I could feel the sweat forming on my palms.

"Vicki! Please, wait up. I'm sorry. I can explain everything," I heard him call out.

"No! Leave me alone!" I yelled back to him.

"I can't, not until after you hear me out," Chris replied as I felt his hand trying to grab a hold of mine.

"Let go of me or I'll scream!" I cried, trying to get out of his grip.

"I will, but I need to explain myself first. Please, just give me two minutes and then if you still want me to leave you alone, I will," he pleaded.

"Okay, but only two minutes. Start talking," I said, keeping my distance.

"Thank you. I don't know why I behaved the way I did but I did and I'm sorry. You just made me so crazy when you wouldn't talk to me back there," he explained.

"That's no excuse! You're not my father, boyfriend, or husband, and even if you were my boyfriend or my husband, it's none of your business. Furthermore, you have no right putting your hands on me like that. By the way, your time is up and I need to get back to my friends," I told him as I started to walk away.

"What the heck is this bologna you're throwing at me?" Chris barked, then went on saying, "What about me? I'm your friend and then some."

"You were a friend, but that was it, nothing more. I don't know where you got the idea that you were something more," I told him.

"I think that I got the idea from the way that we connected earlier and also from that intense kiss we shared," Chris snapped as he grabbed me again.

"The kiss and everything was nice, but you kind of ruined the evening when you began acting like an animal and talking like you owned me," I stated.

"Nice, that's it! You're a real piece of work. One minute you're all over me and then just because I misunderstood a conversation and held your arms too tight, you try to run away from me. You know what you are?" he remarked.

"Yes, but why don't you tell me what you think I am," I retorted back.

"You're a tease and a tramp," he answered.

"Well, you're the biggest jerk that I have ever met in my whole life, and I never want to see you again," I told him as I ran towards the dock.

When I got to the dock, I turned around to see if Chris was behind me, and he was nowhere to be found. I kept my emotions locked up inside of me so nobody would find out about what happened. Luckily Katrina was ready to leave, because I didn't think that I would be able to keep up a front for too long.

"Are you all right, Vicki? Katrina inquired.

"Yes, I'm fine. Why do you ask?"

"It's just I saw you and Chris arguing a few minutes ago and you seem a little upset."

"We weren't really arguing, I just told him how it is, and he didn't like what I had to say. It did upset me a little but I'll get over it," I assured her.

"Well, let's go get our stuff and finish the party up at my house," she suggested.

"Sounds great, but who else is going to be there?" I asked as we headed towards the table where our things were.

"Nobody has to be there if you don't want them to be."

"As long as Chris doesn't show up there, I don't care who's there."

"That's fine with me. I'll go and spread the word to everyone but Chris," she said, walking over to the dock where the rest of the gang was.

When she came back, we began our walk to her house. As soon as we got there, we went upstairs to grab some items for the party. Katrina thought that it might be cool if we slept outside. We grabbed her tent, a couple of sleeping bags, some pillows, and some food and drinks. About a half-hour later, a truck pulled into her driveway. It was Mitch, Warren, and my brother, Matthew. They came upstairs and told us that everyone else had other plans. The guys decided to be gentlemen and carried all of the stuff to the backyard for us. While the guys set up the tent, Katrina and I walked over to the playground at the church next door. We got on the swings and began swinging while we talked about our plans for the future.

"So, Vicki, what are you going to do this fall?" Katrina asked.

"I'm going to college to major in psychology, but I may try to take a few other courses if it's possible. I would like to study art history—antiques—literature, and music," I explained as I jumped off the swing.

"That sounds not only interesting but also time consuming. I haven't really decided what I want to do, but I still want to go to college somewhere and try it out," she replied.

"I'm sure you'll figure it out after you've been there for a couple of weeks or so," I told her, walking towards the monkey bars.

"Yeah maybe, but even if I don't, at least I'll be getting out of this town," she said.

"That's one way to look at it. I don't mean to be rude, but would you mind leaving me alone for a little while? There are some things that I need to think about, and I think well when I'm alone," I asked her.

"Okay. Are you sure?"

"Yes, I'm sure."

"If you need anything, just give a holler," Katrina said as she walked back to her yard.

"Okay, thank you. I'll be over there in a little bit," I replied as I watched her disappear into the shadows.

It was so still and calm that you would almost think time had stopped. There were no cars on the road below or crickets buzzing from the pond nearby; it was all so peaceful. I closed my eyes so that I could enjoy the quietness all around me. All of a sudden, my quietness stopped. There were bushes rustling and the sounds of footsteps coming up behind me. Quickly, I turned around to see who had disturbed my peace. It was Mitch.

"I told Katrina that I wanted to be alone for a little while. I guess I should have also told her to tell everyone else," I said to him.

"She did tell us that you wanted to be alone, but I had to make sure for myself that you were all right. So don't be mad at her, she did try to stop me," he explained.

"Well, now you've seen that I'm okay and everything, so you can go," I told him, turning away.

"You might be physically okay, but you sure aren't emotionally," Mitch said as he came closer.

"What makes you think that?" I asked.

"I can tell not only by the way you are talking, but also by the look in your eyes. They seem so lost and lonely. It's making me crazy," he replied, brushing his hand along the side of my face.

"Please don't do that. How can you tell how I feel by looking into my eyes, and why does it make you crazy?" I asked him, feeling a little nervous from his touch, what he said, and what he might say.

"Your eyes are so beautiful that it seems like such a shame to see them look so sad. If you're feeling this way because of Chris, please don't."

"Why not?"

"He's a lowlife!" Mitch exclaimed.

My mouth dropped, my eyes got big as if to see something extraordinary, and then I said to him, "What would make you say something so cruel about a friend of yours?"

"For one, he is not my friend. Secondly, I know about some of his prior relationships and they were pretty abusive."

"Even if you are telling the truth, some people do change, and I believe in giving people a second chance," I replied.

"Maybe some people do change, but Chris is not one of those who can. I admire and respect your compassion towards people, but it may get you hurt one day," he said, moving closer to me.

"Thanks, but if you don't mind I would like to be alone for a few minutes," I said.

"I'll leave on one condition," he replied.

"And what's that?"

"You dance with me just once."

"I guess I can. If I don't, you probably won't leave me alone."

"You're right. Now close your eyes and let me have your hands so that I can lead you through the moonlight," Mitch said as he began reaching for my hands.

"But there's no music," I told him.

"That's why you need to close your eyes and use your imagination," he replied.

So I let him take my hands in his and we began to dance. I imagined myself dancing across a ballroom floor dressed in a mauve full-length gown. I felt as if were back in the late 1800s to early 1900s when things seemed so glamorous and innocent. His hands moved softly up my arm to my shoulders and then down around my back, caressing every inch. Moving his way up towards my neck, he leaned into me and pressed his lips gently along my neckline.

"This feels so good and right, but I know that it can't be. You're not Chris and—" I started to say as I pulled away from him.

"And what, Vicki?" he asked.

"Nothing, just forget about everything that has been said and done here tonight," I answered.

"I can't and I don't want to forget any of it. The feelings that have started inside of me tonight are like nothing that I have ever experienced before. You can't pretend that you don't feel anything, because I know that you do," Mitch expressed firmly, pulling me back to him.

"First of all, don't you tell me that I feel something if I don't. Next, just because you do, doesn't mean that I have to go along with them," I told him as I sat on a rock behind me. "Lastly, I have a boyfriend and I don't even know if you have a girlfriend or not. In fact, I know nothing about you."

"Calm down, there is no need to get agitated. I'm sorry if I have hurt you in some way, I wasn't trying to," he said, squatting down in front of me.

"You didn't hurt me or anything; it's all just so confusing."

"Well, maybe I can clear the air about a few things. For one, you don't have to do anything that you don't feel comfortable doing or feel something that you don't. And about Chris, I understand that you are kind of with him, but there are things about him that you should know," Mitch replied.

"Like what?" I inquired.

"He has had a history of abusing women that he has been caught cheating on him, and I heard that he really hurt one girl that he was with just for being late. This is the information that I was trying to tell you about earlier, but you were too busy to listen to me. Maybe now you'll believe me after what happened between you two back at the lake."

"Even if you are right, I can handle myself, so don't worry. The only thing you should worry about is the answer to my question."

"Oh really? Go ahead ask away," he chuckled.

"What about you? What deep secrets are you hiding? Who's your girlfriend?" I asked him.

"Well, you already know my name, so I guess that other than the personal stuff, the only thing that I can tell you is that I am a free agent," he answered politely.

"Why can't you tell me more about yourself? Do you have any skeletons in the closet that might be embarrassing?" I questioned.

"No, nothing like that. It's just that I don't usually open up to just anyone," he answered.

"That's fine with me. I was just curious," I said.

"Do you think that we can finish our dance now?"

"No, I have a better idea. Come with me," I replied as I took his hand and led him back to the tents where we were supposed to sleep.

As we crept into the tent, Mitch stopped me in mid motion and whispered, "Why are we back here?"

"Because I'm feeling a little tired and I wanted to feel safe when I fell asleep. Plus I need a blanket and pillow nearby," I told him as I adjusted my pillow and laid my head down.

"Oh, okay." He smiled, lying down next to me.

"Don't worry, I promise to pity and respect you in the morning," I chuckled.

"I hope that you'll respect me, but I don't know why you'll have pity," he said with a puzzled look.

"I'm afraid I snore," I smiled.

"That's okay. I have been known to carry a good snoring tune, myself," he smiled back.

"Goodnight," I said.

"Goodnight," he replied, leaning towards me.

His lips were moving closer to mine; the feeling of anticipation was overwhelming. I was wondering how he would kiss me, with his lips open or closed? Would they be pressed softly or hard? Would he try to slide his tongue into my mouth? Just as I was thinking about his kiss, it happened. His lips touched me, but not where I expected. Here I was waiting for them to be on mine and they end up on my left cheek. Without showing my surprise and disappointment, I pulled away slowly and turned over.

He didn't say anything, nor did I. Maybe he wanted to kiss me but was afraid I wouldn't let him. On the other hand, maybe it's just how it happened and I wanted more. Either way, it was getting late, and I really needed to get some sleep instead of worrying about some guy not kissing me that wasn't even my boyfriend. *Tomorrow I am going to try to patch things up with Chris*, I thought to myself as I drifted off to sleep.

- 2 -
A Long Day

When I woke up the next morning, I wasn't in the tent; I found myself lying in a bed. I heard music and turned to see where it was coming from. Katrina was sitting at her desk listening to the radio next her on the windowsill.

"How did I get in here?" I asked her.

"Mitch carried you in here this morning before he left," she answered.

"What time is it and where is everybody else?"

"It's 8:00 a.m. and the guys left for work."

"Oh, I see," I said, still a bit sleepy.

"I'm surprised that you don't remember being carried in here. You must be one of those heavy sleepers."

"How did he get in without waking your parents?" I asked her.

"Easy, they go to bed with cotton balls in their ears," she giggled.

As we started to laugh about the whole incident, there was a knock at the door. Katrina's mom came in and said, "Vicki, there's a boy named Chris waiting in the den for you. He seems very antsy."

"Why do you think that?" Katrina asked her.

"Because he's pacing the floor," she answered.

"Please tell him that I have nothing to say and don't wish to see him," I told Katrina's mom.

"Okay," she said as she walked back out of the room.

A few minutes later she was back and she didn't seem too happy.

"What's wrong?" I asked her.

"He says that he's not leaving until he talks to you," she answered.

"Then I guess that I will have to go hear what he has to say so there won't be any trouble," I sighed as I walked out of the bedroom and headed for the den.

When I approached the doorway to the den, I saw Chris sitting on the sofa. I went over to the window and looked out so I wouldn't have to see his face.

"Good morning, Vicki," he said.

"What's so good about it, and is that all you have to say to me?" I asked him, still peering out the window across the yard at the tents.

"No, that's not all I have to say. I came here to apologize for the way I behaved last night. What I did was totally uncalled for. I had no right to act like that."

"You're right. I hope that you have learned your lesson so that you won't make the same mistake with the next girl," I told him.

"You mean to tell me that you're not going to give me a second chance?"

"I don't know, let's just see what happens. I'm not making any promises, but one…"

"And what's that?"

"If anything like that ever even comes close to happening again, it will be over for good. I just don't understand why you did it."

"I don't either, I guess that it's because I have never had feelings for a girl like this before. But I promise to try harder from now on," he explained as he came up to me and kissed me on the hand. "Come outside with me for a minute. I have something to give you."

"I'm not going out there in my pajamas!" I stated.

"Oh, come on, you're not in the city anymore. You don't have to worry about weirdos or perverts," he assured me.

"Yes, I do. You're a big weirdo and an even bigger pervert," I laughed while running down the stairs leading outside to the front yard.

I hid behind the door at the bottom of the stairs so that he wouldn't find me. When I thought that the coast was clear, I came out from my hiding spot and went outside to wait. Just then I felt two hands grab me from behind and spin me around. It was Chris; he pulled me to him and said, "Close your eyes." It hadn't been three seconds when I heard him say, "Okay, you can open your eyes now and see how much of a weirdo and a pervert I really am."

"They're gorgeous, thank you so much," I cried looking at the soft pink roses in his hands.

"Yes, they're a mirror image of you," Chris said as he began kissing the side of my face and then working his way to my lips.

His hands moved slowly up and down the center of my back, and the further down his firm hands went, the more I wanted him to explore other areas of my body. I had to stop before it went any further, but how could I end the sensual feeling erupting inside of me?

Then it hit me! *Doesn't he have to go to work or something? I will try that and see if that will work. If not then I will tell him that I have to go and help my grandmother take some trash to the dump.*

Maybe he was thinking the same thing I was, because at that moment he pulled away from me and said, "I'll call you later when I get done helping my uncle out with the roof on the barn." Then he was gone.

As I headed back to the staircase, I heard someone call out to me. Turning my head in the opposite direction, I looked to see where the voice was coming from. It was Mitch and Warren. They approached me with smiles on their faces.

"My, my, look at what we have here. It's a pair of very sexy legs attached to a very nicely shaped body," Warren replied, looking me up and down.

"Cut it out, Warren. You are going to drive me to the point where I won't be able to control myself and I will end up kissing that body from head to toe all day and night," Mitch smiled.

"Now, stop that. You two are making me feel like a cheap piece of meat. Besides, I don't think that Chris would appreciate it much either," I told them.

"He better not say anything," Mitch stated.

"Why not?" I asked him.

"Because, it's his fault for letting you come out here dressed in your pink nightgown. Of course guys are going to look at you like that. In a way, it's also your fault," Mitch answered. "If you did not try to make yourself look so hot, you wouldn't have a problem."

"I will agree with you on that one, bud," Warren said, patting Mitch on the shoulders.

"Well, for your information, I don't have a problem. But, I do have some good news if you want to hear it," I told them.

"Lay it on us, babe," Mitch said.

"First of all, Chris came here to apologize for the way that he acted last night. Now for the reason why I came out here like this; it was so that he could give me these," I replied as I brought the roses from behind me.

"Wow! Those are nice; they almost look like wild flowers," Warren said.

"What do you think, Mitch?" I asked, noticing a look of disappointment come over his face.

"Like Warren said, they're nice," he answered.

Why does he look upset? I thought to myself. *Is it because of the flowers or what?* I didn't know the answer, but I had a feeling that now wasn't the best time to try to get an answer from him.

"Are you guys coming upstairs or what?" I inquired as I began to climb the stairs.

"Yeah, we're right behind you," they said simultaneously.

When I walked into the kitchen, I immediately started telling Katrina and her mom about what had happened downstairs with Chris. Then I showed them the roses that he had bought for me and they both said how gorgeous they were. A few minutes later, I noticed that Mitch and Warren weren't around. I went back downstairs to see if I could find out why they didn't come upstairs. As soon as I got outside, I saw them talking over by the edge of the road. They seemed to be whispering, because I couldn't hear them when I got closer to them, and they were awfully close to one another's ears.

"Hello boys. Aren't we being snooty little liars today," I sneered.

I must've startled them because when I began to speak they both jumped and jerked their heads towards my direction.

"Are you trying to give me a heart attack or what?" Mitch shrieked.

"You shouldn't go sneaking around like that, someone could get seriously hurt," Warren replied.

"I'm sorry; I didn't mean to scare you guys. It's just that I didn't know what had happened to you, so I came to find out."

"I am sure that I speak for Mitch when I say that we are also sorry, we didn't even think about how much time had been passing us by," Warren said.

"That's okay, as long as you tell me what was keeping you," I said.

"I'll let Mitch tell you because I want to get upstairs and see Katrina," Warren replied as he ran back to the house.

"So, tell me the big secret you two have," I smiled.

"I can't tell you," he said.

"Why not?" I inquired.

"Because, it's not something I can tell you. It is, however, something I can give you," he answered, taking my hand in his and leading me over to his truck. "Close your eyes," he whispered.

Not even two seconds later I felt something in my hands. It felt hard and kind of square, almost like a box. The suspense was killing me, when was he going to let me open my eyes?

"You can open them, now," he said.

I opened my eyes, looked down at my hands, and said, "It is a box, and I knew it."

"Well, go on. Open it up."

"Hold your horses," I told Mitch as I pushed his hands away.

The box was about the same size and shape of a boot box. There was an ivory ribbon, which went around the box and tied on top in a bow. Inside was a cream-colored tissue paper with pink and blue roses. This matched the wrapping paper on the outside perfectly. I pulled out a black leather dress that was short and strapless, with a v-neckline in the back and was rounded just right in the front, where it should. There was also a pair of black lace stockings and matching gloves to go with dress. The gloves were short and didn't cover the fingers. I was shocked and speechless. My day seemed to be starting out so well. What could I possibly say to Mitch besides thank you that wouldn't sound selfish?

"Thank you so much. The outfit is gorgeous, but I don't understand why you did this. Believe me when I say that I don't want to sound ungrateful and seem it, but I'm confused and I don't think that I can accept this stuff," I told him.

"You're welcome. I think that I know why you feel the way you do," he replied.

"Oh, you think so. Well, why don't you tell me your opinion?" I said.

"I feel that because of your situation with Chris and what happened last night when we danced, you don't know where to turn. You are caught between a rock and a hard place because of your feelings for both of us," he explained.

"I never said that I had feelings for you," I replied.

"You didn't have to; it was written all over your face a few minutes ago after you opened your gift. Last night I could sense it in the way you were laying next to me," he smiled.

"Even if you are right about my feelings, we can't be together because I am with Chris. I need to give him the chance. It just wouldn't be fair to deny him after I pretty much already said that I would," I explained to Mitch as I began to walk away.

"Wait a minute," he called out to me.

"Why?" I asked as I stopped and turned around.

"Please, accept the gift and give me a chance to prove how happy I can make you," he pleaded.

"I will accept your generous gift, but I don't think that I can oblige you on the other matter. It would be cheating and I am not that kind of girl."

"I understand, but I think that I may have a solution," he smiled.

"You seem to think that you have all of the answers, so clue me in," I sneered.

"Don't be so sarcastic. It's not very ladylike. Anyway, here's my plan. We will go out on a date as friends and see what transpires, if anything."

"I guess that might work, but you have to promise me one thing before I agree to do this."

"Just tell me and it's yours," he told me, reaching for my hands.

"Don't overdo it, you might end up changing my mind."

"Okay, I'm sorry," he said sadly.

"All right, now as I tried to say, I want your word that if I want the date to be over it will be."

"You have my word as a gentleman," he replied as he bowed before me.

"So, with that said, where are we going?" I asked.

"I thought that we would do a little dancing at this club that I know about in the city. Then afterwards we could get a bite to eat at the restaurant of your choice."

"Sounds interesting, but you still haven't told me when all of this is supposed to take place," I replied.

"Well, if it isn't too much of a problem or inconvenience, then I would like to go this Friday. We could leave about seven and get to the club by eight to beat the crowds," he said.

"Then I guess that I will see you on Friday at my place. Don't be late," I smiled.

"Don't worry, I won't be," he smiled back. "Wait, Vicki. I just need one more thing from you. It will help me make it through the long week," he said.

"Hey, now, I told you that I wasn't like that," I said feeling a bit upset at what he had just said.

"It's nothing like that, so calm down. All I want is a hug, that's it," he told me while holding my hand.

"Oh, Mitch, I'm sorry. It's just the way you said that, it sounded like you wanted something else," I replied as my cheeks turned red from embarrassment.

"That's okay, I totally understand. There's no need to feel embarrassed," Mitch assured me.

"Do you still want that hug?" I asked him, looking down at my feet, trying to hide the look of shame still on my face.

His hand gently lifted up my chin, and then he looked deep into my eyes and said, "You know I do. Please, don't be upset, it was an honest mistake. You're only human, after all."

"Thank you for being so understanding." I smiled as I slowly looked up at him.

"You're welcome. Now how about that hug?"

I didn't say a word; I just flung my arms around his neck. Then I pressed my body against his and I could feel his arms wrap around my waist in a tender embrace. We stayed like that for a few minutes, then let go and went our separate ways.

A couple of hours later, Katrina and I decided to go to the beach with Warren and Chris. I called Chris at his uncle's house to see if he wanted to go. He said that he would meet us there in an hour.

When we got to the beach, I began to set up our things near the lifeguard chair while Warren and Katrina raced to the water. Of course, Warren won, but only because he cheated by snapping her bikini top. A few minutes later I was looking around to see if Chris had arrived, and I saw Mitch over at the picnic table with a couple of other people. I decided to go over and talk to them for a while, or at least until Chris showed up.

"Fancy that! I never thought I'd see you here," I said, approaching the table.

Mitch jerked his body around to face me with a look of surprise and said, "Hey, do I know you?"

"Do you know me? What kind of game are you playing?" I asked him, feeling a bit bewildered. *Is he kidding around with me or is he being serious?* I thought to myself.

"I'm not playing any game, but I think that you have me mistaken for someone else," he answered.

"I guess that I was mistaken. You obviously aren't who I thought you were," I said, noticing a cold demeanor on his face.

Instead of sticking around to get humiliated even more, I turned around and ran as fast as my legs could carry me. I ran right past Katrina and Warren without stopping and headed into the woods. What I needed right now was to be alone so I could try to make sense of it all. I found a big oak tree and sat down under it. My mind was racing with thoughts of confusion and sadness. As the tears began to roll down my face, I began thinking about why Mitch was acting like that. *Is he ashamed of our friendship? I thought I meant something to him.* Then it hit me! Could it have been because of the girl that was sitting next to him? Did he lie about not having a girlfriend?

One thing was for sure, our date was off, and it didn't matter to me. Who was I fooling? It did matter, but I couldn't let it. Just then, I heard footsteps approaching from the left side of where I was sitting. I looked up to see Katrina standing next to me.

"What is wrong? Why did you run right past us? And why are you sitting here all by yourself?" Katrina asked.

"Nothing is wrong. I'm sorry if I was being rude by going right by guys without acknowledging you," I answered.

"You weren't being rude, so don't be sorry. I do wish that you would be honest and tell me what's bothering you. I could tell when you ran by and I can tell now by the look on your face," she replied.

"I want to tell you, but that would mean that I would have to admit my feelings. It's just not worth it."

"It is, Vicki. But now is not the time to discuss your problem with Mitch."

"Why not, and how did you know about Mitch?"

"I kind of figured it out, because at the time, he was here and Chris wasn't. Speaking of Chris, he's here. So you need to dry your face and act natural when you see him," she responded as she wiped my face with a tissue from her pocket.

"Thank you, for being such a good friend," I said as I gave her a hug.

"That's what I am here for," she said patting my back. "We had better get move on before he gets suspicious."

We stood up, wiped the dirt off our shorts, and headed back to the beach area. As soon as we got back I immediately ran up to Chris and hugged him. Then I proceeded to kiss him as if hadn't seen him in years.

"Don't take this the wrong way, but what has come over you?" he asked, pulling away from me.

"Nothing, I just missed you so much," I told him, as I hoped that Mitch had seen us a moment ago in our lip lock.

"Let's go for a swim," Chris suggested.

"Okay, but give me a chance to change," I replied.

Before I took my clothes off, I looked around to see if any one was looking. Besides Chris, the only other person that had their eyes on me was Mitch. Good! I wanted him to watch me, and boy was I going to give him a show. First, I proceeded to untie my halter top, and then I slowly took it off one arm at a time. Next, I was going to work on my high-cut jean shorts. I peered over at Mitch and caught his eyes moving up and down my body. Obviously my plan succeeded in getting his attention. When Chris was ready, we put our arms around each other's waists and began walking towards the water.

"You can't catch me, old man," I snickered as I started to run into the water.

"You're going to get it, now. You just wait, lady," he chuckled while chasing me in the water.

Trying to get away from him, I went under the water and headed towards the dock. Not looking where I was going, I bumped into someone. Before I could get a chance to see who it was, the person started kissing me. What a kiss! I thought that it must be Chris because it was so deep and passionate. I opened my eyes and saw Mitch, not Chris. So, I pushed him away and swam away from him as fast as I could. While I was heading up for air, I thought to myself, *Why did he do that? Why risk being seen?*

I gave up on the answer and swam over to a big rock where Chris was waiting patiently. We stayed there for a little while just enjoying the time we had. After we were done relaxing, we swam over to the dock. I started to climb up when Chris bit me in the rear. It didn't hurt too much, but I definitely was going to pay him back. Just as he stepped onto the dock, I pushed him back in the water. Then I did a back swan dive into the water and headed for shore. Everyone began to whistle, cheer, and clap as I walked onto the beach. I figured it had to be because of what I did to Chris, so I smiled. While the sun was still out, I decided it was time to try to get a tan.

I got the lotion out of my bag and was about to put it on when I heard footsteps from behind me.

"Could you put some lotion on my back, please?" I asked.

I didn't feel any hands rubbing my back, the lotion was still on the ground next to me, and I got no verbal response. Wondering what was going on, I turned my head and saw Mitch. There was my answer, but I was still curious.

"What do you want?' I asked him, turning my back to him.

"I want to talk to you, it's important," he answered.

"Oh sure, when you want to talk to me, it's okay. But when I want to talk to you, you say that you don't know me. So, I guess if you don't know me, we have nothing to talk about."

"I understand that you are upset with me, but I can explain everything," Mitch said.

"Good, 'cause I want to hear this lame excuse. Unfortunately, we can't talk right now."

"Why not?"

"Because I am here with Chris, and you're here with your friend there," I answered, pointing towards the direction of the table.

"Okay, set a time and name the place. I will be there no matter what."

"Meet me at my grandma's in an hour. I'll tell Chris that I have to go and help her with something and will be back as soon as I can. I don't like to lie, so you had better show up and have a good reason for what you did earlier," I told him as I stood up.

"Sounds good, as long as no one else is there," he said.

"Don't worry, my grandma is away for the day, and my brother won't say anything. Just worry about your own friends."

"My friends won't be around. Until we meet again," he replied.

A half-hour later, Katrina came up to me and said, "I see that you and Mitch are talking once again."

"We are and we're not. He's meeting me at my grandma's in an hour so we can talk some more."

"I hope you two work everything out. You and Mitch make a better couple than you and Chris," she stated.

"Why don't you spend the night with me?" I asked her as I gathered my things.

"Sure. I have to run it by mom first, just in case. She may need me to watch after my younger brother."

We walked over to the picnic table and told Warren and Chris that we were going to her house for a few minutes. At first, Chris didn't seem too happy with the idea, but when I explained the situation, he was okay. After we asked her mom and got the okay, we gathered her things and headed for my house. When we got there, I noticed Chris standing in the driveway. I gave Katrina the house key and she went in without me.

"What are you doing here, Chris?" I asked him.

"I forgot to give you something. Please, close your eyes," he replied as he walked behind me and began to put his hands near my neck.

I didn't know what to expect, but that didn't surprise me. The way this day had already been going, anything was possible. Suddenly I felt cold metal around my neck; it felt like a chain necklace. I looked down and saw a tri-toned necklace hanging from my neck.

"What is this for?" I questioned curiously.

"It's to show everybody that you're my girl. I want us to go steady, Vicki."

"I can't," I cried as I ran into the house.

"Why?" I heard him yell. Then a few minutes later there was silence.

"Is he gone, Katrina?" I asked her, shying away from the openness of the door.

She looked outside then said, "Yes, I do believe he has left."

Without going into too many details, I just told her that I wasn't ready for a commitment. Then there was a knock at the back door. Katrina went upstairs and I went over and answered the door. It was Mitch, and he was alone.

"What's wrong? Did Chris hurt you?" Mitch asked me.

"No. It's none of your business, anyway. Plus, you have no room to talk about hurting someone."

"It is my business when it comes to you. I know that I hurt you really bad earlier and that's why I am here."

"Whatever, I'm not going to argue about your opinions. I just want to hear your excuse and then you can leave for good," I said sitting down at the kitchen table.

Mitch joined me at the table and then started to tell me his story. "You know how I told you that I didn't have a girlfriend? Well, I wasn't lying to you, I just need to find the right moment to explain everything to you."

"I guess now is as good a time as any."

"Here it goes. Misty, the girl you saw me with at the beach, is my ex-girlfriend. The problem is, she still hasn't gotten over me and she says she never will. We're still friends, and when I get lonely, she's there. I know that sounds cold and shallow, but at least I know that I won't catch a disease from her," he explained as he tried to catch his breath.

"You're right, that does sound cold and shallow. It is also very wrong and stupid on both of your parts. You can't expect her to get over you if you still sleep with her."

"I know, it's just that I don't know what to do."

"Just stop hanging around with her so much. And when you feel lonely, find a distraction or take care of it yourself."

"First, that's a lot easier said then done. Secondly, I don't want to take care of myself; I need a woman for those kinds of needs," he replied.

"Then I guess that you should get a girlfriend."

"You're right again. I think I have found a girlfriend. Unfortunately, she doesn't know that I am alive," he sighed, looking away.

"Well, then you need to do something about it. If you wait too long she might get involved somewhere else."

"Do you really think so?" he asked, turning back around.

"Yes, I do."

"Okay. Then I better do it right away," he replied.

"Good luck!" I exclaimed.

"Thank you," he said, and then he walked out the door.

Well, there I was, sitting in the kitchen all by myself. Two men that I cared deeply for had left me and had done so all on the same day. I was just heading into the parlor when I heard a knock at the door. *Maybe it's Chris*, I thought to myself. I opened the door and there was Mitch standing there with a smile and a white rose.

"What are you doing back here? I thought that you were supposed to be winning some poor girl's heart," I asked in amazement.

"I am trying to, if you would let me."

"What are you talking about?"

"You really don't know?" he smiled.

"No, I really don't."

"You're the one, Vicki. You are the woman I have been dreaming of my whole life," he said, taking my hand in his.

"You're kidding, right?" I gasped.

"No, I'm not. I knew from that night when we first met and we danced under the stars. I love you so much that words could never totally express how I truly feel about you," he replied.

"But I don't understand. How can this be?" I started to say, but stopped due to an overwhelming sensation that was running through me.

"I know exactly how you feel. That's the way I felt before I knew what had happened," he stated. "You love me, too. Don't you?" he questioned.

"I don't know. I feel like I do, but I don't. I am so confused," I said, getting up from the table.

"Please, Vicki, don't pull away from me. I can help push that confusion out of your life if you'll let me," he replied, pulling me down to him.

"How can you take away these clouds in my brain and in my heart?" I asked him as the tears slid down my cheek.

"Vicki, please, don't cry. It hurts me to see you suffering like this. Let me ease all of your pain, right here, right now," he pleaded.

"I just—" I started to say, but Mitch interrupted by pressing his soft, thin, wet lips against mine.

Our lips locked in a passionate kiss. I sat on his lap and threw my arms around his neck, rubbing every inch. He put one of his hands around my waist and the other between my legs. His lips moved gently down my neck, while he gently caressed my inner thigh. I was tingling all over. My body felt so out of control, like a time bomb ready to explode.

I moved one of my hands down his back to his firm buns and then proceeded to the front of his body. That's where I knew I could really turn up the heat. His breath felt so hot on my neck. I could feel his heart pulsating through his clothes. It was like rain hitting a tin roof, and I'm sure that mine was about the same.

We were going at it in the kitchen for about a half-hour when Mitch stopped. He put his hand on my chin, turned my head to face him, and then said, "I don't want to stop, and I want to make love to you more than you know. Nevertheless, I think that we should wait for that special time. Besides, I still have to prove to you that I am the better man."

"I was afraid to stop in a way, because I thought you would be upset. Anyway, you may not have to worry about proving yourself a better man," I told him, moving over to another chair.

"Why is that?' he asked.

"Well, because Chris wants to go steady and I don't. He left when I told him that I couldn't," I answered.

"He might have just gone somewhere to let off some steam," Mitch explained. The telephone started to ring from in the parlor.

"Hello," I said as I picked it up.

"Hi, sweetheart," the voice on the other end whispered.

"Oh. Hello, Chris," I responded, looking over at Mitch.

"What are you doing? How are you?" Chris asked.

"I'm fine. I was taking a nap," I answered.

"Oh, 'cause you seemed upset when you took off into the house, earlier."

"I have to tell you something," I said to him.

"What is it?"

"I'm pregnant," I answered and noticed a look of shock on Mitch's face.

"Whose is it?" he asked loudly.

"It's nobody you would know. This was from before I came up here," I told him.

"You had better get an abortion or else!" Chris yelled into the telephone and then hung up.

"I can't believe he reacted that way. That was just so cold," I said.

"I can't believe that you're pregnant and this is how I am finding out," Mitch stated.

"I'm sorry. I wasn't planning to tell anyone when I first got here. It's just something that I didn't want to deal with right now," I explained.

"Talk about being cold. You don't even want to deal with this," he said coldly.

"You just don't understand; it's not that simple. I won't know for sure until next week," I told him.

"Sure, okay. I don't want to pressure you or anything. I hate to break things up, but I have to go to work. I'll talk to you later," he replied as he kissed me and then left.

Katrina came downstairs and we talked for a while. Then my Grandma came home and made dinner for us. We had beef stew and biscuits for a main course and gingerbread and whip cream for dessert.

"Victoria, I have some mail for you," Gram said to me as she walked into her office.

"Here it is. It came from Rhode Island," she said, handing me a manila envelope.

I opened it up and there was a letter and a small envelope inside. The letter read:

> *Dear Miss Whitley,*
>
> *We heard that you were going to Maine for the summer, so we took it upon ourselves to send you the tickets for the rock-n-roll benefit that you requested. There is a concert in Portland on Wednesday, the twenty-first. When you get there, just show them the badge that is enclosed and you will still get front-row seats and backstage passes. We have already informed the managers and the supervisors, so they will be expecting you. Good Luck!*
>
> *Sincerely,*
> *The Crew at 96.5 WLJY*

"Yes!" I screamed as I leapt out of my chair.
"What's all of the screaming about?" my brother asked as he walked in from outside.

- 3 -
The Concert

"We don't know," Katrina told him.

"Calm down, Vicki. Tell us why you are screaming?" Gram questioned.

"I got two front row tickets to a rock-n-roll benefit that is going to be in Portland this Wednesday. Plus, I have backstage passes for after the show," I explained with a smile.

"How did you get them?" Katrina asked me.

"I ordered the tickets a couple of months ago. The passes must have been a prize in some contest, and I guess that I won them," I answered. "Do you want to go with me, Katrina?"

"I'd love to. First, I have to make sure my mom doesn't need me that night," she replied.

She called her mom to find out if she had to babysit Wednesday. Her mom said that she didn't need her Wednesday, but did need her Tuesday and Thursday. After we finished eating, we watched a little television. Afterwards, we went out back to listen to some music. When we danced off all of the food that we had consumed, we headed for bed. It had truly been a long day and one that I would always remember.

A couple of days had passed and I hadn't seen or heard from Mitch or Chris. Then, just as I was walking into town, I heard a car come screeching behind me. It was Chris. He pulled off to the side more but didn't shut off his car.

"Hey, Vicki. Get your rear in gear and get in the car!" he yelled.

"Why are you yelling at me like that?" I asked him as I neared the car timidly.

"You lied to me!" he said raising his voice even louder than before.

"Please, don't yell at me. You're really starting to frighten me," I cried.

"Good!" he hollered.

"Why are you so mad at me? What did I lie about?" I asked him.

"You told me that you were pregnant and your not. I checked with every hospital and clinic, and they all said the same thing: that you had never been there for any test," he scowled.

"I never said that I went around here. To be perfectly honest about it, I'm not sure and won't find out until next week. I am truly sorry if I hurt you; it was never my intention. Maybe it's better this way. I have made mistakes, and so have you."

"What mistakes have you made?" he asked, getting out of the car.

"It's not important, so just leave it alone. It's my problem and I have to deal with it. You need to deal with your temper," I explained as I reached for his hand.

"You think that I have a temper? Baby, you haven't even seen my temper. And if you think that you are going to just dump me, well, you have another think coming," he replied as he began punching me in the face, smacking my head, kicking me onto the ground, and calling me all sorts of horrible names.

"Please, stop! Chris, I'm sorry! You're hurting me!" I begged and pleaded as much as I could for him to stop. He just kept on hurting me repeatedly. If this is what it felt like to be hit by a Mack truck, then I can really feel for all of those dead animals on the freeway.

I prayed to God to give me strength and peace, and if possible to send me some kind of help. My prayers were answered; everything stopped as I said, "amen." I looked up from my crouched position and saw Brian, Danny, and Paul standing over me.

"It's all right, Vicki. You don't have to be afraid or worry about Chris anymore," Brian said.

"We just happened to be passing by when we heard your cries for help and saw what was happening," Paul said.

All three of them carefully lifted me up and carried me over to the grass. The pain was excruciating and the tears were pouring down my cheeks. Nothing like this had ever happened with a boyfriend before. *What did I do to be punished like this?* I asked myself.

"Just hold on a little while longer, Vicki. We are going to take you to the hospital as soon as Brian comes back with his car," Danny said to me while wiping my tears and holding my hand.

When we arrived at the emergency room entrance, the nurse on duty came out with a wheelchair and brought me into a room. Within five minutes, the doctor had me rushed to the x-ray room, the lab, and the bathroom for a urine sample. I don't think that it was in the exact order, though. When they were done with all of the exams and x-rays, they brought me back to my room. Due to the hospital rules, Brian, Danny, and Paul were not allowed in the room because they were not family.

About an hour later, the doctor came into my room and said, "Miss Whitley, you have sustained some minor cuts and bruises on your arms, legs, and back. You have slightly bruised ribs and a cracked jaw on the left side of your face."

Then he wrote out a prescription for some Motrin and gave me some ointment to put on my bruises and for my jaw if it became swollen. After they were done wrapping my ribs with bandages, Brian came and wheeled me out to the car. He returned the wheelchair to the ER, stopped to talk to the nurse, and then came out.

"Vicki, I don't know if you know what this means, but the nurse told me to tell you that the test turned out positive," Brian said with a puzzled look as he started the car.

"Yes, I know what she's talking about. It's just some test about iron deficiency, that's all," I assured him.

I hated to lie to him, Paul, and Danny, but I couldn't tell them the truth. At least, not until I figured out exactly what I was going to do and when. They drove me home and explained to my grandmother what had happened with Chris and everything at the hospital. I really wasn't up to talking or anything, so I went upstairs and tried to get some rest. Most of the time that I laid in bed was spent thinking about what had happened. It still felt like a nightmare and I wished that it was and not an actual event. Finally, I began to drift off and fell asleep.

The next day I woke up and it was about 11:00 a.m., which meant that it was time to get up. While I was in the middle of nibbling on a piece of wheat toast and jam, the phone rang. I walked slowly into the parlor and answered it.

"Hello," I answered.

"Hello, yourself. What's up?" the chipper voice on the other end of the telephone replied.

"Hi, Katrina. There's a lot up, but I'll explain later," I said, then paused for a moment to think. "What are you doing today?"

"Nothing yet," she answered.

"Can you meet me at the beach in about an hour?"

"Sure," Katrina said.

"I need to go to the store to pick up an Instamatic camera, some film, and flashes, okay?"

"That's fine, we can go together,"

"Cool, I'll see you up there."

"Yep, bye," she replied.

"Bye," I replied and then hung up.

I stuffed the toast in my mouth as I walked upstairs to be dressed and packed up. When I finished getting ready, I went to my grandmother's room to ask her for a ride.

"Gram, if you're not too busy, do you think that you can give me a ride to the beach?" I asked as I sat on the edge of her bed.

"Do you think that's a wise idea?" Gram asked, walking over to the closet.

"I know that you are worried about Chris coming after me again, but don't. There will be plenty of people there who won't let him near me," I explained, trying to reassure her and myself.

"I'll do it, but only if you promise to call the police and me if anything happens," she stated.

"I promise, Gram," I told her as I placed my hand over my heart.

"Let me get the keys and use the bathroom before we go," she said, walking over to the night stand where her keys were.

"Okay, I'll get my stuff and meet you in the car. Thank you very much, Gram," I replied as I gave her a hug.

"You don't have to thank me, dear. Just be very careful."

"I will."

She left the room and went downstairs while I went to my room and grabbed my stuff. On my way out the door, I remembered my medicine that I had left on the counter. I picked it up and stuffed it in my tote bag, then went outside to the car. My grandmother came right out right after I did and we left. As I got out of the car when we reached the beach, my grandma told me not to forget my promise. I reassured her that I wouldn't and she left. Just as I started walking over to the restroom, I heard a girl's voice calling out to me. I stopped, turned around, and saw that it was Katrina.

"Hey, Vicki. Wait for me!" she yelled to me from the other end of the parking lot.

"I am!" I yelled back.

"Were you going to the store without me?" she asked as she caught up to me.

"No, I was just going to the bathroom. You can come if you want to," I told her as I started to head over to the bathroom.

"Oh, okay. I'll come with you," she smiled as she started walking with me.

"In fact, I'm glad that you are coming with me. That way I can tell you about what happened yesterday," I said to her.

"What are you talking about? What happened?" she asked, puzzled.

"Come inside with me, first," I told her when we reached the bathroom.

"Hurry! I don't want anyone to see us or hear what I am going to tell you," I said, waving her inside. "Before this goes any further, I need you to make a vow of silence," I said to her as I closed and locked the door behind her.

"I swear on my soul that I won't say anything unless you tell me to," Katrina replied.

"Okay, here it goes," I said as I took off my coat to show her my wounds.

Her eyes nearly popped out when I pointed out my cuts, bruises and bandages. She looked like she had seen a ghost the way her face went white. "Oh, my goodness!" she said hysterically. "What the heck happened to you?"

"Chris is what happened to me," I responded.

"What do you mean? Were you two in a car accident?" Katrina inquired, still looking at my wounds.

"No, it definitely was no accident."

Instead of going into the long and gory details, I just summed everything up quickly. I told her about our argument on the telephone, and then informed her of my walk into town. I told her about how he beat me over not telling him about my possible pregnancy and how I thought that we should end our relationship.

"You mean to tell me that he did all of this over something that had nothing to do with him, and you feeling that you two were better off without each other?" she asked in shock.

"Yes."

"Oh, Vicki, I am truly sorry this happened to you. If there is anything that I can do to help, please, let me know," she cried as she reached out to hug me.

"Please, don't cry. You're going to get me going and it hurts my jaw too much," I pleaded as I pointed to my jaw.

"I'm sorry!" Katrina exclaimed, hugging me again.

"That's okay. Let's not get all worked up over this and ruin our day," I told her, putting my big Mickey t-shirt on over my bathing suit.

"You're right, let's have some fun. In fact, I have some wine coolers back at the blanket in my cooler," she smiled.

"Oh," I pouted as I turned away from her.

"What's wrong?' she asked.

"I'm not supposed to be drinking any alcohol, remember?" I said, pointing to my tummy.

"OOPS! I forgot all about that. I am sorry."

"I know, it's hard for me to remember as well."

"Don't worry, I won't ask who the father is or anything. It is none of my business or anyone else's for that matter," she stated as she rubbed my back.

"I just don't know what to do. I want to tell someone about it, but I'm afraid," I sighed.

"Don't be. You have a lot of friends here who care about you," she said, hugging me.

"Thank you. I hope so, cause what I am about to tell you is something big," I said.

"How big could it be?"

"This is bigger than what Chris did to me. You may want to sit down or hold on to something," I told her, pointing to the bench near the door and the sink next to her.

"All right, if you say so," she said, walking over to the bench.

"About a month ago, something happened to me down the road from my house," I said.

She must've guessed what it was, because her head dropped to her hands and she began crying. I walked over to her and sat down next to her, trying to comfort her. She sat right up and held onto me, still crying.

"Vicki, I am so sorry. I don't even know what to say. I have never met anyone who went through that before. The guy who did this should burn in @*#^!" she cried.

"He's in jail, at least for the time being. I hope that you don't think different of me now that you know," I replied.

"Heavens no! You did nothing wrong!" she shrieked.

"Please, don't say anything to anyone about this," I pleaded.

"I promise," she said, crossing her heart with her hand. "What are you going to do about the baby?"

"I haven't really decided yet. It all depends on my family, finances, and if Mitch will still wants me when he finds out," I told her.

"I can understand about your family and the finances. But, why does it also depend on whether or not Mitch will still wants you?" she questioned, putting her hands on her sides, looking like a mother giving a lecture.

"Because I think that I love him and I don't want to lose him over this," I explained.

"You won't be alone. Your friends and family will be there for you. However, I do understand what you're saying about Mitch. All you can do is tell him and wait to see his reaction. The number one thing to do is pray," she replied.

"I know you're right. Now that all of that is out of the way, let's go over to the blanket," I said, picking up my stuff.

"That's the spirit. You deserve some rest and a little bit of fun," she smiled, holding my hand.

We left the bathroom and walked over to the blanket. I had just sat down and gotten comfortable when I looked up and saw Mitch striding towards me. He sat down next to me on the blanket and asked Katrina if he could have a few moments alone with me. She went over to a table that was only a few feet away and sat down.

"I heard about what happened with Chris. Are you okay?" he questioned.

"Not really. I am still shaken up over the whole thing. I have a cracked jaw, cuts and bruises on my arms, legs, and back; and bruised ribs."

"I am so sorry. I wish that you would have listened to me before and then none of this would have happened," he said, then paused for a moment while looking at my wounds. "I'm sorry, that was uncalled for," he said putting his arm around me.

"That's all right; you didn't really know what he was capable of. I don't think that he even knew or knows," I told him.

"Don't defend that turkey! I could say something else, but I won't," Mitch stated angrily.

"Believe me, I'm not. Getting off that part of the story, I have something else that I need to tell you," I said as I clenched my hands together.

"What is it?" he asked.

"Well, I don't know how to tell you, and I'm not really sure if I should. But, I will give it a try." I hesitated, then blurted out, "I'm pregnant!"

He started breathing heavy as he stood up and began looking around on the ground.

"What's wrong?" I asked him.

"What's wrong, you say. That's funny," he sneered.

I was starting to get scared again, and I guess that Katrina could tell, because she stood right up and came to my defense.

"Mitch, please calm down. You're scaring me," I cried out to him.

"I hope you don't expect me to stay with you and support this child. For one, it's not mine. Secondly, I am not the daddy type. So, I guess if you want to be with me, then get rid of it!" he yelled.

"How can you be so cruel after everything that has happened? After all that you said to me, why are you doing this to me?" I asked as the tears began streaming down my face. I couldn't believe what I had just heard him say. He is no better than Chris.

"I have one last thing to say to you, and then I am out of here. It's very easy to do this. You need to forget about us, because I am going to," he sneered as he turned and walked away.

This felt like déjà vu. Yesterday I was asking myself, *why?* My mind and heart were doing topsy-turvy spins and I couldn't deal with it. I just wanted to run and keep on running, never stopping or looking back.

"Vicki, are you okay? Of course, you're not. How stupid of me! How could I even ask such a question?" Katrina said, sitting next to me.

"Katrina, I can't handle any of this. I just want to end it all," I cried as I buried my face in my hands.

"Don't talk like that. Nothing or nobody is worth killing yourself over. What you need right now is to get out of here for a while," she stated, trying to help me get up.

"And go where?"

"I have my mother's car, so we'll go to the store and then for a ride. It'll be a long ride to wherever you want."

"I don't feel up to going anywhere, though," I told her as we walked over to the parking lot.

"You don't have to; I will go in for you. All you have to do is sit in the car and wait," Katrina replied while helping me into her mom's Chevelle.

"As long as you don't mind, I'm game," I said softly.

"I don't," she said, starting the car.

When we arrived at the store, I handed her a list of things that I wanted and I gave her some money to pay for it. Before she left, she asked if I was sure that I would be okay out here. I told her that I would be fine and she went in. A few minutes later I started getting upset again. I got out of the car and walked towards the entrance of the store. Just as I was stepping onto the sidewalk, everything went black.

The next thing that I remember is many voices around me. I opened my eyes and saw at least five people hovering over me. Katrina was there, as were couple of people that I didn't recognize, and one who I definitely knew. It was Cody Williams of the rock group the Falcons. He was their drummer. *What is he doing here, in this small town?* I thought to myself, forgetting about what was going on at that moment.

"Are you all right, Miss?" he asked.

"Vicki, can you hear me? Are you okay? What happened?" Katrina asked as she tried to pick me up.

I came back to reality and stood up. Nodding my head, I told her that I was fine, then said, "I started to get upset and when I tried to walk over to the entrance, I guess I fainted or something."

"Vicki, can you see okay?" Katrina inquired.

"Yes," I replied.

"It did look like you had fainted or something. I saw you fall and came right over," Cody Williams said.

"Well, thank you for being here, sir. I think that I can handle it from here," Katrina said as she looked him over.

He eyed her right back and smiled, "You're very welcome. Your friend looks like she needs to go to the hospital," he replied.

"No, she'll be fine. She just needs some rest and a calmer life."

"Why, what's wrong?" he inquired.

"It's nothing for you to worry about. Thanks, anyway," she answered, walking me back to the car.

"Katrina, do you know who this is?" I asked her.

"No. Should I?" she questioned.

"Yes. He's Cody Williams, the drummer for the Falcons. They have been my favorite rock band since I was about five," I smiled.

"You're kidding, right?" she asked.

"No, she's not. I am Cody Williams," he said, extending his hand out to greet her.

"I can't believe that you are standing right in front of me. My name is Katrina Smith," she giddily replied, taking his hand and shaking it.

"And I'm Victoria Whitley," I said, shaking his other hand.

"Would you two lovely ladies like to go somewhere and talk?" he asked us.

"We'd love to," Katrina grinned.

"You can follow us over to the beach. We'll find a secluded place where nobody will disturb us," I said to Cody as I got in the car.

"Sounds like a plan, let's go," he responded.

"Okay. We'll see you in a few minutes," Katrina said, getting in the car and starting it.

Cody walked over to his car, got in, and started it. The engine sounded so sweet; it purred like a cat. He had an early model, black-top thunderbird. We pulled out of the parking lot at the same time and headed over to the beach. They parked their cars next to each other under a big oak tree. We walked into the wooded area of the beach and sat down under some willow trees. It was the perfect hiding spot. Katrina and I explained the whole story about Chris, Mitch, the pregnancy, and me. It was so unexpected and weird to be telling somebody famous our predicament. What was even stranger was that he was actually listening.

"I can't believe the things that someone can go through and in such a short time. I am truly sorry for all that you are going through," he said when I had finished with my story.

"Thank you, but there is no need for you to feel sorry for me. I'll get by somehow," I told him, although I didn't believe it myself.

"I'm sure you will. Maybe there is something that I can do to make your day a little brighter," he said while scratching his head for an idea.

"You don't have to do anything; you've done enough just by being here," I assured him.

"But I want to," he told me.

"Don't argue with him. If he wants to be nice, then let him," Katrina said, nudging me.

"All right, I'll keep my mouth shut and appreciate Cody's kindness," I sighed.

"I got it!" he exclaimed.

"What do you 'got'?" Katrina asked.

"An idea," he answered her. "Are you ladies going to the concert tomorrow night?"

"You bet. We have tickets and backstage passes," I told him.

"Oh, well, there goes that idea," he moaned.

"That's okay," Katrina replied.

"Yeah, it's the thought that counts," I told him.

He stood up, paced back and forth for a while, then turned to both of us with a smile and said, "I have a better idea."

"What?" I asked him.

"I can't say right now, but I'll let you know tomorrow night when you're backstage," he answered.

"Ooh. It sounds like a big secret," Katrina smiled.

"No, it's not really a secret. I just want to confirm it first," he replied.

"Okay. On that note, I think that we should get going," I suggested to them.

"Why?' Katrina asked.

"Because I'm sure that Cody has places to be right now," I explained.

"As a matter of fact, I do have to get back to the studio," he said.

"I do have one question for you before you go," Katrina stated.

"What's that?"

"Why did you come here, of all places?"

"It was my turn to get the refreshments, and I thought that a small town would be the safest place to go."

"I guess you were wrong," I said to him.

"Why do you think that?" he asked me.

"Because you ended up having to deal with us, and I'm sure that is the last thing you wanted to do," I answered.

"Don't say or think that. I'm glad that I met you and Katrina," he smiled.

"Really!?" Katrina exclaimed.

"Yes, really."

"Thanks for everything, Cody," I said, giving him a quick hug.

"No problem," he said, hugging me back.

"What about me?" Katrina asked him with a smile.

"I didn't forget about you," he smiled as he walked over and hugged her.

We said our goodbyes and went our separate ways. Katrina and I decided to go for a quick swim. We walked over to the dock and jumped into the water. I didn't do anything too harsh except for one dive and a cannonball. After a while, I started to get tired and Katrina said she would take me home. I also guessed she probably had plans with Warren later that night.

As we pulled in my driveway, she turned to me and said, "If you need anything, just call me."

"Thank you, but I think I'll be fine. I'm probably just going to go straight to bed."

"You do look worn out," she replied as I slowly got out of the car.

"I feel it. Well, I guess that I will talk to you later. Have fun tonight," I told her, walking up the front steps.

"Yep, bye!" she called out as she drove off.

I did exactly what I said that I would do. After I changed into my nightgown, I went straight to bed. Later that night, I woke up from a bad dream, crying and sweating. I don't really remember too much about it; however, I do remember dying in a house fire.

Morning came and I felt a little more rested than the day before. I didn't really feel up to eating, so I got dressed and went downstairs. My grandmother was sitting in the parlor knitting a blanket when I walked in.

"How are you feeling this morning, dear?" she asked, not looking up at me.

"I'm feeling much better," I told her, sitting down across from her on the rocker.

"That's good. Then I take it you and Katrina will still be attending that concert tonight?" Gram inquired.

I threw up my hands and said, "I completely forgot all about it. It's no wonder with everything that has happened over the past few days."

"Well, don't fret. At least you realized it in time. Maybe you and Katrina could go to the mall and get an outfit for later," she hinted.

"That's a great idea. Besides the fact that I have nothing to wear, it's also a great way to kill some time," I replied. "But, I have two slight problems," I sighed.

"What are they?" she asked, still knitting and not looking at me.

"I don't have a way there and or any money. I won't have money until next Tuesday when my mom sends it to me."

"I think I can solve both of your problems."

"How?" I questioned.

"I'll lend you my credit card and my car, but on two conditions."

"Oh, Gram, you don't have to."

"I know, but I will. Now listen, you have to fill the gas tank before you bring it back, and don't crash it. Now about the credit card, try to stay under a hundred dollars, okay?"

"Okay. Don't worry; I will do everything that you said. Thank you so much, Grammy," I smiled as I ran up to her and hugged her.

"You're welcome, dear," she said, kissing my cheek.

"I am going to call Katrina and see if she wants to go with me," I told her, walking over to the desk where the telephone was.

The telephone rang about three times before someone finally picked up and said, "Hello."

"Is Katrina there?" I asked the voice on the other end of the line.

"Yes, hold on," the voice said.

While I waited for Katrina, I tried to figure out whose voice that was. I couldn't figure it out, and then I heard Katrina's voice on the line.

"Hello," she said.

"Hey, girl. What are you doing today?" I asked her.

"Not much, just sitting around," she answered.

"You should be thinking about what you're going to wear tonight," I told her.

"Why? What's tonight?' she questioned.

"I guess that you forgot, too. It's the night of the concert."

"Oh yeah, that's right. I did forget."

"That's okay, so did I, the reason I'm calling is to see if you want to go to the mall with me. My grandmother is lending me her credit card and her car," I told her.

"That's cool. Sure, I'll go with you," she replied.

"Well, if you're ready, then I'll come and get you," I said to her.

"I'm ready whenever you are," she said.

"Okay, I'll be right there," I said and then hung up.

After I picked Katrina up, we headed for the mall in North Conway, New Hampshire. When we arrived there, we had trouble finding a place to park because the mall seemed to be extremely busy. About ten minutes later we found a spot in the middle of the lot and parked. Since it was around noon, we decided to get something to eat before we shopped. We went to a sub shop and got a couple of Italian subs, chips, and two bottles of water. I didn't finish everything, so I put my leftovers in a bag for later. The first shop we went to was Deb's. It had a nice variety of casual and formal wear. There were so many outfits to choose from that it was hard to pick just one.

I knew that my outfit had to be neutral. It had to be classy and casual. Ten outfits later, I finally found the perfect ensemble.

It was a short, black, strapless and low cut dress that had a matching blazer. With or without the blazer, I could get that neutral look. It was perfect! Now it was time for my accessories and shoes. A black choker and a matching onyx bracelet and earring set would accent the outfit perfectly. All I had left to get was a pair of shoes and maybe a purse. I paid for the outfit and jewelry and then we walked over to the shoe store. It didn't take as long to find shoes as it did to find the dress. The shoes I wanted were on display in front of the store, right next to the purses. The shoes and purse were a perfect match. Both of them were black with clear sequins on a satiny material. The sequins on the open-toed heels went along the lining that went around the top of the foot. In addition, the sequins on the purse went along the outer lining.

It was getting late and we still had to get ready. We left the mall and I sped home. Normally, it would have taken us about an hour and a half, but this time it only took about fifty minutes. As soon as we pulled into the driveway, we made a dash for the door.

I took a shower first while Katrina looked through my closet for something to wear because she wasn't sure about the outfit she had brought at mall. The outfit she bought was a cream-colored spandex mini-dress. If she had a matching blazer, or even a short cotton coat, that would've looked good. When I got out of the shower and went upstairs, she was still looking.

"I can't believe that you still haven't found anything," I told her.

"Nothing looks right," she replied.

"What about your outfit with my cotton blazer?" I asked her as I pulled it out from the closet.

"I guess that I can try it on. I'm sure that it won't look right," she grunted, taking it from me.

I turned around so that she could change her clothes in peace. It didn't take her long to change; a few minutes later she told me she was done. I couldn't believe my eyes. She looked gorgeous! She was definitely going to turn some heads at the concert.

"Wow! You look so gorgeous," I told her with a big smile.

"You're kidding, right?"

"No, I'm serious. I knew it would look good on you," I replied.

She looked in the mirror hanging on the back of the door and said, "I guess you were right. Thank you."

"What for?"

"For letting me wear this coat, pushing me to try it on, and for the compliment."

"You're welcome."

"Enough gabbing, let's finish getting ready," she said.

"Finish? I haven't even begun to start!"

First, I put my undergarments, dress, blazer, and shoes on. Then, while my hair was drying in the towel wrapped around my head, I did my make-up. Because I was wearing an earth-tone colored outfit, I picked out matching make-up. *Now for my hair, how am I going to have it?* I thought to myself. After careful consideration and a lot of mousse, I finally decided to put my hair in a French bun. I twisted it in the back and then pinned it. All that was left was my jewelry. Out of everything I had to do, I think that was the simplest thing.

When we were both finally done, we looked each other over and smiled. We agreed that we were both going to turn heads. Katrina went downstairs to use the bathroom while I went to say goodbye to my grandmother.

"Have a good time, dear. Please, be very careful on the road and at the concert," she said while embracing me.

"I will on all counts, I promise."

"Okay, goodbye."

"Goodbye," I said, walking out of her room.

I met Katrina outside in the car after I made sure I had everything. It was about 5:35 p.m. when we left my grandma's house. Portland was about an hour away and the concert wouldn't start for another two hours. That meant that we could take our time. The traffic was even good, which was a surprise for that time of the day.

We arrived at the music hall early enough to get a good parking spot. I put the tickets and pass in my purse, then locked up the car and went inside. I showed the usher our tickets and passes; he looked them over and then motioned us to move forward. We had decent seats that were in the middle of the seventh row from the center of the stage. A few minutes later, the show started with a soloist doing a collection of different pieces. First, he did an operatic aria (song) without music. Then he did a beautiful piece on the piano. There was something about him that seemed so familiar, but I couldn't place what it was.

For the first part of the concert, all they played was classical music and opera. At intermission, the emcee announced that the Falcons would be next to play. Katrina and I decided to go powder our noses and get something to drink while we had the time. That's when I caught another look at that soloist from earlier. It was driving me crazy that I couldn't remember who he was. I felt like I was trying to find a needle in a haystack. The only way to solve my problem was to go up to him and find who he was. My solution fizzled, however, when I noticed a beautiful and tall blonde walk up to him.

"What's wrong, Vicki?" Katrina asked.

"Nothing," I answered.

"You can't lie to me. I can tell by the look on your face.".

"You're right, I'm sorry. It's just so frustrating," I sighed.

"What is?"

"Not being able to remember someone that you know."

"Who's here that you think you know?"

"Do you see that man over there next to the beautiful blonde?" I asked her as I pointed to a man standing next to a woman in the doorway to the concert area.

"Yes, I see him. That's the soloist from earlier. That's probably why you think you know him," she responded.

"No, that's not it. I know him from somewhere else."

"Well, then, if you can't remember, just go up to him. You can act like you're lost or something. Then if you get a good enough look at him, maybe you'll remember who he is," she suggested.

"I can't do that. I'll feel stupid. Let's just forget about the whole thing and get back inside the auditorium."

When we got back, the Falcons had already begun playing. They played all of their old songs and a couple of newer ones. A few times, the lead singer would stop singing and talk to the audience about the reason for everyone being there tonight. By the sound of the clapping, I would say that most of the audience was here to listen to the Falcons.

At 10:30 p.m. the show ended and everyone was leaving. An usher came up and took us to where we were supposed to go backstage. It was a good thing too, because I would've been lost for hours. When we walked into the dressing room, it was empty. At least, there were no groupies. We sat down on a sofa near the door and waited for the Falcons or someone to come in. Just then, the door opened. It was Cody.

"There you are. I have been looking all over the place for you two," he said, trying to catch his breath.

"We've been here for a few minutes," Katrina told him.

"Well, come with me and I'll introduce you to the rest of the band," he suggested as he motioned us over to him.

"That's what we came here for," I replied, getting up off the sofa.

We walked across the hall and into another room. There, standing by a coke machine, was Luke Nash, and of course, the rest of the band.

"Vicki and Katrina, I would like to introduce you to Luke Nash, David Blithe, and Simon Tayler. Guys, this is Katrina and Vicki," Cody replied.

Everyone shook hands, said hi, and then sat down on the chairs that were scattered around the room.

"Cody told me you were attractive, but I don't think he gave you enough justice. You are beautiful," Luke said to me with a smile.

"Thank you," I replied, feeling a little warm around my face.

"You're welcome. By the way, Cody also told us about what's been going on in your life. I am very sorry, and if there is anything that I can do, or the rest of the band, just let me know," Luke told me as he handed me a card with their telephone number on it.

"Thanks, that is very kind of you," I said, putting the card in my purse.

It was getting late, so I told Katrina I was ready to go. She wasn't ready to go, but she did for my sake. Luke walked us out to the car to ensure our safety.

"I wish you all the luck in the world with this problem of yours. Remember; call me anytime you need to," he said, shaking my hand.

"Thank you, maybe I will," I told him.

"If you decide to get an abortion, I can help with that, too. Even if it's just a ride to the clinic," he replied.

"I really appreciate your kindness, thanks again," I said.

"No, problem," he said as he pressed his lips against my cold and trembling lips.

As he kissed me, his hands caressed my hair and the back of my neck. I wanted to run my hands through his long strands of midnight curls, but I couldn't. Fear was flowing through my body and I didn't know what to do except pull away from him and leave as fast as I could. Neither one of us said a word; I got in the car and left him standing there.

On the ride home, conversation was very scarce. I didn't say anything to Katrina and she didn't say anything to me. When we returned home, I turned to her and asked, "Do you like Cody?"

"Yes, but I also like Warren," she answered as she stepped out of the car quietly.

"You could always date them both," I whispered to her as we neared the front step.

"I don't know if I could do that," she replied.

- 4 -
Humiliation

"All that you can do is try. At least if you try it, you won't be able to say that you regret not trying it," I told her, tiptoeing into the house.

"Maybe, you could be right. But, it also depends on if Cody likes me or not."

"That's true."

"What about you and Luke?' she asked as we crept upstairs.

"What do you mean?" I asked, walking into my room.

"You know what I mean. The kiss that you two shared before we left," she smiled.

"Oh, that. It was just a harmless kiss, nothing more," I reassured her, although I wasn't so sure myself.

"Well, like you said, try it. You never know, it just might work out between you two."

"I have a suggestion. Let's both just drop the subject. Neither one of us is getting anywhere."

"Okay, I'll say nighty-night and then keep my mouth shut," she chuckled.

"I will, too," I giggled.

"Nighty-night, Vicki."

"Night-night, Katrina."

We both kept our word and didn't speak another word for the remainder of the night. I got my nightgown on and hopped into bed, while Katrina put her nightshirt on then hopped into the bed next to me. For some reason, I woke up earlier than Katrina, so I went for a jog. When I came back, I jumped into the shower to clean all the sweat off my body. Just as I was getting out, there was a knock on the door. I put a robe on then went to the door and opened it.

"Is Victoria Whitley here?" a short, thin young man with sun-fire hair asked.

"Yes. I am Victoria," I responded.

"Well, then these are for you," he replied as he brought from behind his back a bouquet of flowers.

"Is there a card?" I asked him.

"It's inside there," he answered, pointing to the middle of the bouquet.

"Thank you. This is for you," I told him as I handed him a five-dollar bill for a tip.

He thanked me with a big smile and then left. I closed the door, and then reached inside the flowers for the card to see who had sent it. As I sat down at the kitchen table, I opened the card and began to read it. It said, "I'm sorry for hurting you and I hope that you will forgive me. I love you. Chris." It was a sweet gesture, but I couldn't forgive him. What he did to me was not only unforgivable, but also unbearable. It's something that will stay with me for a long, long time. I wanted to call him and tell him how I felt, but I knew deep down inside that I would get the same reaction as before. I decided that if I didn't call him, he would get the hint.

Mitch was going to be another one that I was going to avoid at all costs. He behaved just as badly as Chris did, except there was no physical abuse. Not yet, that is. *Am I doing the right thing?* I thought to myself. I needed to talk to someone who didn't know much about the situation. The only person that even came close to fitting that description was Luke. First, I had to call the clinic to make an appointment so that I could talk to a counselor about my pregnancy.

I called the clinic and they made an appointment for me to come in next Monday. Then I called Luke at the number that he had given me.

"Hello," the voice said on the other line.

"Hi. Is Luke there?" I asked.

"Yes, hold on and I'll get him for you," the voice replied.

There was a moment of silence. Then I heard, "This is Luke."

"Hi, Luke, it's Vicki. I hope that I'm not bothering you or anything," I mumbled.

"No, not at all," he declared.

"Good. I just needed some advice from an outsider," I told him.

"Okay, what's the problem?" he inquired.

I briefly explained to him about Chris wanting a second chance, and how I didn't want anything more to do with him. Then I told him that I felt the same way about Mitch. Before I could say anymore, he interrupted me.

"I think that what you are trying to do is not only smart, but very courageous, as well," he expressed softly.

"You really think so?"

"Yes, I do. It takes guts and brains to do what you're doing. I wouldn't worry about Chris coming after you again. I don't think he'll want to mess with me and my friends," he declared.

"Thank you so much," I replied gleefully. "I don't know what else to say."

"I do. Say that you'll go out with me tonight."

"Sure, I'd love to."

"I'll be there at about 6:00 p.m. Wear something casual. If you want to, you can wear the outfit that you wore last night," Luke suggested.

"Okay, I'll be ready when you get here," I said.

"All right, see you then."

"Yep. Bye," I replied, hanging up the telephone.

Time had gone by so fast that I didn't even realize that it was almost six o'clock. Luckily, I had already taken a shower, so all I needed to do was throw my clothes, then do my hair and put some make-up on. I took his advice and wore what I had on last night. I was just finishing up my make-up when Luke showed up. After the final touches, I went out to the kitchen where Luke was patiently waiting. He was dressed in a pair of khaki slacks, a beige knit sweater, a pair of cowboy boots, and a matching cowboy hat.

"You look very nice," I told him.

"Thank you. You don't look so bad, yourself," he smiled.

Then my grandmother walked into the kitchen, so I introduced Luke to my gram and vice versa.

"Luke, this is my grandmother. Gram, this is Luke. He's the lead singer for the Falcons," I explained.

"Hi, how are you tonight, ma'am?" he asked her while shaking her hand.

"I'm fine, thank you for asking," she replied, and then asked him, "How are you? Where are you taking, Vicki? And, when will you be back?"

"I'm good. We'll probably go out for dinner, and then head over to the recording studio for a while. I'll bring her back safely around midnight," he answered politely.

"Don't you think that's a little late for her to be out in her condition?"

"Well, I guess—"Luke started to say but I interrupted him.

"Gram, I'm twenty years old. I think that I'm old enough to make my own decisions," I snapped.

"Don't take that tone with me, young lady," Gram demanded.

"I'm sorry, Gram. I know that you care and everything, but you're treating me like a child."

"While you are staying in my house, I will treat you however I want. Especially if you show me no respect."

"Fine!" I yelled as I stormed out of the house.

I got into Luke's pickup and turned on the radio. *Why did she have to do that to me in front of Luke? I haven't been doing anything that would make her say that. It's just not fair*, I thought to myself as the tears trickled down my face.

"Are you all right, Vicki?" Luke asked me as he got in the truck.

"No, I'm so humiliated and angry. Lately everybody has been treating me like they own me, and I'm sick of it," I cried.

"Don't worry, everything will turn out fine," he replied, putting his hand on mine.

"You're always so positive, I wish I was."

"You will be someday," he said as we drove off.

"I hope you're right," I said, lighting up a cigarette.

"I don't want you to be upset with me, but I feel I have to say that you shouldn't be smoking in your condition."

"I don't even know if I'm keeping the baby, so don't worry about it," I told him, taking a puff.

"I see your point, but still."

"Let's just drop the subject, okay?"

"Okay. I brought you out to have a good time, and that's what we're going to do," Luke replied as we pulled up to the studio.

"I don't mean to sound rude, but what about dinner?"

"It's your choice on that. We can go out to eat or get take out."

"Actually, I'm not hungry right now," I said, stepping out of the truck.

"Well, when you are, just let me know," he smiled.

As soon as we got inside, Luke told me that I could sit in the recording booth while they did their sound-check. I wasn't the only one in the booth. Their manager, recorder, producer, and David's wife were there too. A few minutes later they decided to take a break before they started recording their new song. I told Luke that I needed to use the restroom; he showed me where it was, and I headed in that direction. I didn't really need to use the restroom. What I really wanted was to be alone for a while. I found a room that was full of instruments and equipment, so I went in.

After long thoughts on the past few weeks and about my future, I came to a decision about the pregnancy. It was a hard decision, but I knew that it was the right one. With that out of the way, I headed back to the booth.

"Hey, I thought that you had to use the restroom," a voice from behind said.

I turned around to see Luke walking up to me.

"I'm sorry that I lied, I just needed to be alone for a few minutes," I explained.

"If we're going to try to start a relationship, don't you think that we need to be honest with each other?"

"Well, excuse me!" I snapped, throwing my arms in the air, then said coldly, "I wasn't aware that we were."

"There's no need to cause a scene," he replied, calmly putting his hands on either side of my arms.

"Get your hands off me. If you want a scene, I'll give you one," I shouted, pushing him away from me.

I wasn't even going to give him a chance to respond physically or verbally. I turned around and started to run away from him. I could hear him calling out to me as I went outside, but I wasn't going to stop. My feet were getting tired, so I slowed my pace down to a brisk walk. *Is it Luke that I'm mad at or something else? What he said about us starting a relationship did take me by surprise. Maybe I jumped the gun a bit, but I am getting so tired of people making decisions for me. That seems like what he was doing,* I thought to myself.

A few feet away from me there was a bar, and as I approached the window, I noticed it was very busy. It was the perfect place to rest my feet and try to hide. If Luke did show up, I could either con some help from any number of men that were there or hideout in the ladies room. When I got in the bar, I headed straight for the counter to get a drink. That's when I noticed him. A very well built, fair-haired man sitting there and motioning me to join him. *How can I refuse such a delightful-looking man?* I asked myself as I walked over to him.

We didn't even introduce ourselves, we just started talking and doing shots of tequila. After we did our fifth shot, he asked me if I was ready to do some fancy footwork. I told him yes and we staggered to the floor. As we were dancing to a top-forties song, I began feeling the muscles on his arms and his chest. Then he leaned closer and began kissing my neck and lips. I pulled slightly away from him, looked up at him with a smile, and said, "If we keep this up, the smoke alarms will go off."

He just laughed as he pulled me back into him. All of a sudden, I started feeling very intoxicated, so I walked off the dance floor and went back to the counter. The next thing that I recall, I was up on the counter dancing for a handful of men. Then the man I danced with earlier grabbed a hold of my waist, and proceeded to lay me horizontally on the counter. As I lay there feeling numb, some guys began pouring beer down my throat and caressing my thighs.

For some reason, I felt like I was enjoying the attention from all of the men around me. It didn't seem to matter what they were doing. After all the alcohol that I had consumed, I didn't care. The man I had met earlier lifted me off the counter and sat me on his lap. He wrapped my legs around his waist and pressed his lips firmly against mine. Then, from behind me, I felt someone's hands around my waist and pulling me off him. I opened my eyes to see Luke standing there with a disturbed look on his face. I don't even know how I could recognize him when I felt the way that I did, but somehow I did.

"What in the world are you doing here?" he shouted.

"Why are you talking so loud?" I asked, laughing abruptly.

"I'm shouting because it's noisy in here."

"Well, you don't need to. I'm standing right in front of you."

"Are you going to tell me why you came in here and why you're half-cocked and behaving badly?" Luke inquired.

"I'm not half-cocked. I'm just a little on the tipsy side, that's all. And to answer your other question, I feel that I am behaving just fine."

"You might say that now, but come tomorrow you won't feel the same way. I guarantee it."

"Maybe I will, or maybe I won't. Either way, right now, I don't particularly care," I said, staggering to my seat.

"Come on, I'm getting you out of here," he said, taking my hand and pulling me out of the bar.

As soon as the fresh air hit me, so did the nausea. I stopped walking for a second, and that's when everything I drank tonight came rushing out like a flood. When I was done vomiting, Luke carried me to his truck and sat me in it. Before he even got in on the other side, I passed right out on the seat.

When I awoke from my fainting spell, I found myself in what appeared to be a hotel room. My head was still spinning like crazy and I think I was still a little tipsy.

"You're awake," I heard someone say.

I sat up, looked around, and saw Luke sitting on a chair across from me. As I tried to get off the bed, I asked him, "What am I doing here?"

"I brought you here to sober up," he answered.

"I don't need to sober up. I need another drink," I told him, walking over to a little refrigerator on the other side of the room.

He followed me, then stood in front of me and said, "No, you don't. What you need is a shower, some black coffee, and more rest."

"You don't have a clue as to what I need," I snapped as I tried to get by him.

"Yes, I do," he said, picking me up and carrying me over to the bathroom.

"What do you think you're doing?" I questioned as we entered the bathroom.

"Giving you a shower," he replied as he put me in the shower stall and turned the water on.

At first, the water was cold as ice. Then he put the hot water on to warm it up a bit. My body quivered from the change in temperature for a few moments.

"Are you feeling any better?"

"I'd feel better if you would get me a robe," I scolded.

"Okay, I'll get you one."

I reached my hand out of the shower and grabbed a towel hanging nearby. Then I began drying off while I waited for Luke to come back with a robe. Just as I was wrapping the towel around my head, Luke had walked in.

"Here you go," he said, handing me a long, white, terrycloth robe.

"Thank you," I replied as I took it and put it on.

"You're welcome. I'll be in the other room while you change back into your other clothes," he told me, walking out of the bathroom.

"Okay, I'll be right out."

Instead of putting my clothes back on, I decided to keep the robe on. Then I walked into the other room and asked, "Luke, when and how did my clothes come off?"

"I took them off when we got in the room while you were still passed out."

"So, I gather that you saw me in the buff," I chuckled.

"No. Not really. You see, I had the lights off, so I really couldn't see anything," he explained, and then he noticed I was still wearing the robe. "How come you're not dressed?"

"Wait a minute; I have another question for you."

"What's that?"

"If you took my clothes off and didn't see me naked, then how did you not see me naked when you carried me into the bathroom and into the shower?"

"You didn't notice or feel the blanket wrapped around you?" he inquired as he put his back to me.

"No, I guess I didn't," I replied, feeling a little dazed about the whole thing.

"Now, that I have answered your question, maybe you can answer mine," he hinted.

"Sure. I just didn't feel like wearing my clothes."

"What do you feel like wearing?" he asked, opening a dresser drawer.

"Well, if you turn around, I can show you," I responded while taking the robe off.

"What are you—?" he started saying as he turned and stared at me.

"Cat got your tongue," I laughed.

He turned away from me and said, "Please put the robe back on. You're not yourself right now, and I don't think that you really want to do this."

"Yes, I do. I want you to look at me and do anything else that you want to do," I told him as I turned his head back around.

"No, you don't mean what you're saying," he replied, closing his eyes.

"What's the matter with me? Why can't you look at me?"

"Nothing, that's the problem. I find you very attractive and I don't want you in a position that you'll regret later."

"I understand, but all you have to do is look," I assured him.

"No. You're drunk and vulnerable right now," he stated, walking over to the bed.

"You told me before that if I ever needed or wanted something, you would help me out. Well, I need for you to look at me."

"I know, but—"he started to say until I interceded.

"But, nothing. Just do it," I stated as I strutted over to the bed where he lay.

"If it will end this whole thing, then I will," he replied, turning over to face me.

Luke watched me as I grew closer and closer. He never once took his eyes off me. Looking at him watching was like looking at a lovesick puppy. The way his eyes attached to my body was like a magnet. As I crept seductively onto the bed and closer to him, I could feel the heat from his body on mine.

"Well, by the look on your face, I can tell that you like what you're seeing," I smiled, and then asked, "Am I right?"

"Yes," he gasped, licking his lips.

"That's good. I'm glad you are pleased with what you see. I can give you so much more if you would let me," I replied seductively as I crawled on top of his firm and idle body.

"What are you doing, Vicki?' he asked softly.

"Shh! Just go with the flow and enjoy it," I whispered to him while caressing his chest.

His mouth started to move as if he wanted to say something. Without hesitation, I quickly pressed my lips against his. He didn't resist; he just moved his hands to my back and pulled me closer to him. While our lips remained locked together, I slid my hands behind him and pulled us up to a sitting position. Then I wrapped my legs around him and moved my pelvis closer to his navel. Our bodies began to move in a rhythmic and passionate dance. I pulled away just enough so that I could put his hands on my chest if he didn't. Somehow, he knew what I was thinking, because his hands moved gently to my breasts. He began to softly clutch them while moving his lips down towards them. Sensations were exploding inside of me when his lips touched my ribs.

After a few more minutes of foreplay, he moved me off him and pulled his pants down. Our bodies moved together like symphonic poem. We were like harmony and melody in synchronicity. It was such an awesome feeling and one that I had never experienced before. All of a sudden, things got a little faster then it stopped and he pulled away. I didn't understand what had happened, but I was too tired to find out. He rolled over to the other side of the bed and said goodnight. I knew then that something was wrong, but I couldn't bring myself to say anything. My body longed for sleep, so I closed my eyes and drifted off.

The next morning, I woke up and found myself in bed with Luke. My head was pounding, my stomach was turning, and I had no recollection of the night before. Mortified and fearful at the thought of what could have possibly happened, I quickly and quietly got dressed, then left without a word to Luke. I reached into my purse to see how much money I had, and to my surprise, there was three-hundred dollars. *Where did it come from? Did Luke give it to me? Did I steal it?* I thought to myself. The night before was such a blur that I could have done anything and wouldn't remember. The question at hand was what to do with the money? I did need it, and it was in my purse, so I decided to keep it.

The next thing I needed to do was call my grandmother. I found a payphone, called her, and asked if she could come get me. She said that she would after I told her that I would explain everything when she arrived. I knew it would take some time before she showed up. I chose to pass the time by going into a little shop nearby to purchase a gift for her. It was a quaint place with a variety of items to pick through. She had held a deep passion for red cardinals for as long as I have known her. Up on a shelf over the counter was the perfect gift for her. It was porcelain statue of a mother cardinal and her child on a tree branch. The price was within my budget, so I bought it. The store owner wrapped it in tissue paper, put it in a box, and handed it to me.

As I was coming out of the store, I saw my grandma parked out in front of it. I got in the car and told her that we needed to talk right away. She agreed with me, and then added, "We can go out for lunch if you want."

"That sounds nice, but I'm treating," I emphasized.

"Are you sure that you have enough money to do that?"

"I am positive." I assured her by showing her the money that I had come across.

She drove about five miles then stopped at a drive-in restaurant. After we ordered our food, I handed her the gift that I had bought her.

"You didn't have to get me anything," she said cheerfully.

"Yes, I did. You have done so much for me, and besides, after the way that I acted yesterday, I felt you deserved something."

"That's what I'm here for. Yesterday is totally understandable because of all the stress that you have been under lately."

"Thank you for being so understanding and forgiving," I said as I leaned over and gave her a hug.

Our food came, so we ended the conversation for the time being. On the drive home I briefly filled her in on what happened the night before and when I awoke in the morning. There wasn't much to tell her since I didn't remember much about it, myself. At first, she didn't utter a word. Maybe she was in shock and couldn't say anything. Then, without warning, her silence lifted.

"You're a big girl, now. You've made some mistakes and now you have to take responsibility for them."

"I know you're right. I'm going to start by keeping my appointment at the clinic next week."

"Good for you. If you need a ride, I'll take you."

"Thank you, Gram. I'm not sure yet if I will need you to take me. I'll let you know as soon as I know."

It was about six o'clock when the car slowed into the driveway. As my grandma shut the car off, she turned to me and said, "I love you, Vicki. I am truly sorry that you have to go through all of this."

"Thanks for caring, and I love you, too," I replied, leaning over to kiss her cheek.

When we walked in the house, my brother, Matt, told me that Katrina, Mitch, and Chris had called earlier. I didn't feel like talking to anyone, so I didn't return any of the calls. For some reason my body felt drained, but I didn't want to go bed yet. Instead, I lay on the sofa and watched some television for a while. It wasn't too long after laid down that I could feel my eyes getting heavy. I wasn't certain if I could make it upstairs, so I grabbed a blanket from the closet and lay back down on the sofa.

- 5 -
The Accident

My weekend was okay, but it could've been better. Friday and Saturday I went to a beach in Naples with my brother and my grandmother. At the end of both days were the same routines. We'd come home, have supper, watch some TV, play video games, and then go to bed. Sunday was boring because it rained all day. My brother went to a friend's house, while I stayed home and cleaned. I guess that I still wasn't ready to talk to anyone. That evening was the same as the rest of the weekend: eat, watch TV, and sleep.

I woke up the next morning and looked out my window. It appeared to be sunny outside, so I put on my jogging outfit, and went for a run. Fortunately, it was early when I set out on my jog. I wouldn't have to worry about bumping into anybody. When I reached the beach, it was vacant, which was fine with me. As I bent over to do some stretches, I saw a thousand-dollar bill just lying on the ground. The cat had not only gotten my tongue, but also part of my brain. Part of me wanted to do the right thing and take it to the police. There was also a part of me that wanted to keep it for myself. That kind of money could help me start my life on the right track.

It was settled, I was going to keep it. I felt guilty, but told myself that I would make up for it later down the road. The first thing that I was going to do was buy myself a car. On my jog up to the beach, I remembered seeing a car dealer, so that's where I was heading. The salesman gave me a good deal on a black mustang. It needed some minor work, but for five hundred dollars, I wasn't going to complain. He gave me temporary plates and a temporary inspection sticker, that way I could drive to the registry. After all of the paperwork was completed and I got the keys, I headed to Daniel's house to have him look at it for me.

Daniel told me that he would fix it up and return it to me later. I thanked him and headed home. Nobody was there when I arrived, so I jogged back into town towards Katrina's house. By the time I reached her place, I was out of breath. From my house to hers, I'd say was about a ten-mile hike. When I reached the top of the stairs in her hallway, I saw her hunched over near the front door.

"Katrina, what's wrong?" I asked, sitting down beside her.

"Warren broke up with me," she sobbed.

"Why did he do that?"

"He saw me and Cody kissing in his car," she sighed, trying to collect herself.

"Oh, I see. I'm sorry, but maybe it's better this way."

"Yeah, maybe you're right," Katrina sniffled.

"I know it hurts now, but in time you'll be able to look back and laugh."

"Getting off the subject a bit, I have a question for you," she stated.

"If it's about why I haven't called or anything, I can explain."

"No, it isn't about any of that. I'm sure that you had your reasons."

"I do. Some things happened last week with Luke and I don't remember most of them," I explained.

"Are you saying that you two could've had sex, and you don't remember?" Katrina inquired.

"Basically, that's what I'm trying to say. There is also a period of time that night after I left him at the studio."

"Let me see if I understand all of this. First, you were at the studio and then you left, right?" she posed.

"Right," I agreed.

"Then anything after that is a total blur?"

"You've got it. As I said, the last thing that I recall about that night is when I left. The next thing I knew, it was morning and I was in bed with Luke."

"Were you naked?" she asked.

"Yes, that's why I think we slept together."

"Maybe you didn't, and even if you did, there's nothing to feel ashamed of," she said, patting my back.

"If we did and I was aware of it, then it wouldn't bother me so much.".

"The only way to solve your problem is to ask Luke," Katrina suggested.

"You're right. I'll call him when I get back."

"Where are you going?" she asked.

"I have an appointment at the clinic today."

"Does that mean you're getting the abortion?"

"I'm not sure. That's why I need to talk to one of the counselors before I make my final decision."

"Now that you have answered the question that I was going to ask you, I have another one," she stated.

"You're full of them today. But that's okay, because I'm full of answers," I chuckled.

"Would you like some company?"

"I was hoping you would want to go."

"Do you mind if Cody comes with us?"

"No. Not at all. The more the merrier," I giggled.

"Good. We were planning on a day at the amusement park. Maybe you can come with us after your appointment," she hinted.

"Sounds like fun, which is probably what I will need afterwards."

"In fact, we can invite Luke. It'll be like a double date or something. Plus, it'll give you two a chance to talk things over," Katrina smiled.

"As long as you call and invite him."

"That's fine with me. You wait here and I will be right back," she said as she got up and walked into the kitchen.

My knees began to shake, butterflies filled my stomach, and my heart was racing at the thought of the events that lay ahead for the day. It wasn't long before Katrina was back and telling me that the boys would arrive shortly. About an hour later, Luke and Cody showed up in Luke's truck. We greeted one another and then left for the clinic. I opted to sit in the back of the truck so that I could avoid a big discussion with Luke. It just didn't feel like the right time to talk about that night. Katrina sat in front with Luke and Cody, which didn't bother me.

I was a little late when we got to the clinic, which was okay because they weren't ready for me. When they were ready, a nurse came out and took me into the office. She explained to me my options and then left to get a counselor. The counselor that came in reminded me of my mom. She was short with long black hair and soft green eyes. The one difference between them was that the nurse was a little on the heavy side.

"Have you made your decision?" she asked me.

"I don't think that I can kill an innocent life," I told her.

"I understand, and it's okay to feel like that. As long as you are aware of the responsibilities involved in caring for a child," she explained.

"I am."

"There are resources available to help you and your child. I will give you a list of them if you want."

"That's okay. I will be going back home soon. My mom will help me with all of that stuff," I informed the nurse.

"I'm glad to hear that you have some support. Good luck with everything," she replied, shaking my hand.

"Thank you."

"Just out of curiosity, is the father around?"

"No, he isn't. The situation is rather complicated, and I'd rather not discuss it."

"I understand. Well. Have a good day, Miss," she responded as she left the room.

When I walked into the waiting room where Katrina, Cody, and Luke were waiting, Katrina came up to me and hugged me.

"What's this for?" I asked her.

"Do I need a reason to hug my best friend?"

"No," I smiled.

"Don't keep me in suspense any longer," she stated. and then asked, "What happened in there?"

"Nothing happened. I couldn't do it."

"You did the right thing, I just know it," Katrina declared.

"I hope so," I mumbled.

"Let's not dwell on what-ifs, instead, let's go have some fun," she cheerfully replied.

The guys didn't say anything; maybe they thought that it was best that way. As I got in the back of the truck, Luke asked me if he could join me. I shrugged my shoulders and looked away from him.

"Please don't give me the silent treatment. We need to talk about some things," he pleaded.

"I know, I just don't know where to start," I told him.

"We could start by talking about what just happened back at the clinic," he suggested as we drove away.

"Nothing happened. I decided to be a mother and not a murderer," I told him, looking away.

"Are you sure that's what you want?"

"Yes."

"How will you be able to handle taking care of a baby?"

"I am going back home soon. My mom will help me if I need it. I don't wish to discuss this anymore, so please, no more questions about it."

"Just one more and then I will drop it."

"That's it, and I mean it."

"How are you getting back home?" he inquired.

"I just bought a car today. So, I'll be using that."

"You bought a car!" he exclaimed.

"Oh, I guess that I forgot to tell anyone about it. You see, I was stretching up at the beach when I found a thousand-dollar bill on the ground. So I took it, and that's how I got the car. It's a black mustang. Now, I have a few questions for you," I told him.

"Okay, go ahead and ask away," he replied.

"First of all, did we have sex the other night? Second, did you give me three hundred dollars that night? Third, do you know what I did after I left the studio that night? Finally, why are you here with me?" I inquired, breathlessly.

"Yes, to the first three questions. In addition—"Luke started, but I stopped him.

"We did have sex!"

"Yes, you don't remember any of that night, do you?' he questioned.

"No, that's why I asked you those questions. I don't recall anything after I left the studio and went in that bar," I answered.

"Well, I can tell you what I saw when I came into the bar and when I took you back to my room."

"Maybe what you saw in the bar will fill in the rest," I theorized.

"Here it goes. As soon as I walked in the bar, I saw you up on the counter dancing while a handful of guys stood around watching and drooling. Then you were sitting on this rugged guy's lap while intensely kissing one another. At that point, I knew that I had to get you out of there, so I did. That's when I brought you to my hotel room to sober you up," Luke recalled, trying to get his breath.

"I can't believe that I did all of that. It just doesn't sound like me," I replied, and then thought to myself, *This can't be true, he must be lying. But why would he lie?* I felt horrified, ashamed, and filthy.

"That's not all, there's more," he said to me.

"I don't think that I want to hear anymore. I feel so humiliated," I humbly replied, scooting away from him.

"Well, you shouldn't feel like that. It happens to everyone at one point in his or her life. That's what happens when you drink more than you can handle," he explained softly.

"Obviously I can't handle more than a couple of drinks," I retorted, then turned to him and asked, "I'm probably going to regret asking this, but I need to know. What exactly happened between us at the hotel?"

"You had passed out in my truck, so I carried you into the room, shut the lights off, took your clothes off, and put you in bed. When you woke up, I carried you into the shower to sober you up. After you had finished your shower, you came out in the robe that I gave you and began making provocative advances towards me," he disclosed, and then added, "To make this story end quicker, I couldn't resist your sensual actions and we made love."

"I feel sick," I moaned as I hung my head over the side of the truck.

"It's probably a mixture of the pregnancy and a bad hangover," Luke consoled, putting his arms around me.

"Please. I just want to be left alone for a while," I told him, shrugging his arms away.

"I understand," he said, pulling away.

When we reached the amusement park, I asked Katrina to stay behind with me for a few minutes. The guys told her that they would wait for us at the admissions gate. I told her about my conversation with Luke, and she seemed a bit confused. The color in her face faded, her eyes widened, and she put her hand over heart.

"I know. It was a bit of a shock to me, too," I told her.

"In a way, but I'm more surprised that you're still alive. You must've consumed more than a couple of drinks. Besides, if Luke hadn't shown up when he did, who knows what might've happened to you," Katrina replied.

"I don't even want to think about that. I will tell you that I am leaving soon."

"Why and where?"

"I can't stay here and try to raise this baby with everything that has happened. It would be better if I went home where I can get help from my mom," I explained, hoping that she would understand.

"I can't really say that I blame you. I just wish that we would be able to see more of each other and that none of this ever happened," she sighed.

"We'll still be able to see each other, just not every day. I'll call and write as much as possible," I assured her as we embraced.

"I will keep in touch with you, as well," she smiled.

"Okay, now that we have let our emotions out, let's go have some fun," I suggested cheerfully.

"Let's go," she said.

As we neared the gate, we noticed a flock of girls surrounding Cody and Luke. Luke motioned us over to them.

"Girls, I would like for you to meet two very dear friends of ours," he told the groupies—which is what they appeared to be—as he pointed to Katrina and me.

"You two are so lucky," they screeched.

"Yes, they are," Luke snickered.

"What's that supposed to mean?" I asked in amazement.

"Just what I said," he sneered as he winked at me.

"Do you have something in your eye or what?"

"No, I'll explain later," he whispered to me.

"Later isn't good enough. If you were trying to imply that we are so fortunate to be graced with your presence, then you're sadly mistaken."

"There's no need to make a scene."

"You are very unappreciative, Miss," a girl from the crowd said to me.

"You have no idea about whom or what I am, girlie. If you think that we are so lucky, then I pass the luck onto you. Let's go, Katrina. I'm feeling nauseated being around these lucky clowns," I sneered, taking her hand and walking away.

"I'm glad that you got me out of there when you did. I was about to punch every single one of them, including Cody and Luke. The way that they behaved was intolerable, arrogant, and disgusting," she scowled.

"I agree with you one hundred percent. That's what we get for being associated with rock stars," I told her.

We chose to drop the subject and have some fun. There was plenty do; it was just a matter of finding the right fun. In my condition, I couldn't go on too many rides, which put a damper on things. We walked around for a while, gambled away some of our money at the prize booths, and ate lots of fried food. As we were leaving the restroom, Katrina pointed towards the roller coaster and a couple of guys that were standing in front of it.

"Are you trying to point out the guys or the ride?" I asked her, looking over that way.

"The guys," she answered, still pointing at them.

"What about them?"

"They are staring over here at us."

"Let them, I have had enough of the male species for one summer."

"Don't look now, but they're walking over here," Katrina replied as she turned her head.

"So, I'll tell them that we're not interested," I stated, still facing their direction.

The two guys approached us with smiles. One of them was short and underweight; he had dusty blond hair, green eyes, and an olive complexion. The other one was taller, had more muscles, brown hair, blue eyes, and a paler complexion. They both appeared to be friendly, though.

"Are you two girls here alone, or do you have huge boyfriends lurking in the shadows?" the shorter one asked us with a chuckle.

"We were with a couple of friends, but they had other plans."

"Do you mind if we accompany you girls around the park?" the other one asked, looking at Katrina.

"No, not at all," she smiled.

"I think an introduction is in order, first," I replied, nudging Katrina.

"You're right, as usual. My name is Katrina, and this is my friend, Vicki."

"It's nice to meet both of you," the taller one replied, shaking our hands. "I'm John, and this is my brother, Jimmy."

"Hi. It's nice to meet you," Jimmy smiled, shaking our hands.

"Wait a minute," Jimmy retorted, and then added while looking right at me, "Do you have a sister named Ariana?"

"Yes," I answered.

"I know you and your sister," he smiled.

"How do you know us?"

"We went to the same school. I was in an art class with your sister."

"Now, I remember. You're the short Italian that she talked about all of the time. She said that you had a crush on her," I laughed.

"Oh, she did," Jimmy chuckled.

As we began reminiscing about the old days, Luke and Cody walked up to us. They started pushing Jimmy and John around, while saying simultaneously, "Get your slimy bodies away from them."

"Who are you to tell us what to do?" Jimmy asked as he tried to regain his balance from the push that Luke gave him.

"We are their dates," Cody answered, looking sternly at John.

"Don't go spreading lies," I stated.

"Yeah, you guys aren't our dates," Katrina replied, snubbing Cody.

"That's not true," Luke said.

"Would you guys mind escorting us away from these imbeciles?" I asked, while smirking at Luke.

"No. We wouldn't mind at all," Jimmy happily responded.

"See you two half-wits in another lifetime," Katrina chuckled.

"Hopefully, we won't," I scowled as we walked away.

Jimmy and John knew a shortcut through the park, so we took it, and left the park grounds. As soon as we reached John's van, we hopped in and headed for my house. We were about one or two miles down the highway when a car raced past us. The car disappeared, and we figured that whoever it was must've been in a hurry. John's van was just turning a corner when something hit us from behind. It hit us so hard, that the van went down into a ditch and flipped over. All I remember seeing or hearing were loud sirens before everything went black.

When I came to, I was in a hospital. My vision was a bit fuzzy, but I could see some things clearly. I peered around the room and saw Katrina, my grandmother, my brother, Mitch, Warren, Jimmy, John, Luke, Cody, and the rest of the band standing in front of my bed.

"You're awake, thank goodness. You had all of us worried sick," my grandmother cried, walking over to me.

"When I heard what had happened, I thought that I had lost you for good," Mitch said.

"I am glad to see all of you, but if you don't mind, I need to be alone for a bit," I told everyone.

Everyone nodded, and then started walking out of the room. As Luke reached the door, I called out to him and asked, "Could you stay with me for a few minutes?"

"Yes, but only if you're sure that you're up to it," he answered, turning back around.

"I'm sure. There are some things that I need to tell you."

"Me, too," he said, sitting down on the edge of the bed.

"I'm sorry about earlier, at the park and everything," I cried.

"You have nothing to apologize for. Everything that happened today and tonight is my entire fault." He slowly neared me, as tears began filling his eyes.

"Why are you crying?" I inquired. "We were both behaving immaturely today. There's no need to cry. I'm fine. It's not like you were the one that hit us."

"I'm sorry to be the one to tell you, Miss. But, your friend here is the one who hit the vehicle you were in," a voice called out.

I looked up to see who had said such a horrible thing, and saw a police officer standing in the doorway.

"Luke, please tell me it isn't true. Tell me that it's all a lie," I implored of him as the tears trickled down my face.

He didn't say a word, just sat there looking down at his feet like a remorseful puppy. Just then, Mitch walked in and charged over to Luke with his arms extended out in front of him. The cop stepped in front of Mitch and held him back.

"Boy, you are so lucky that this cop is here, or I would be all over you like flies on fly paper. You're also lucky she had that abortion or you'd really get your tail end kicked," Mitch scowled.

"Stop it! I didn't get the abortion!" I shouted to Mitch.

He stood there in shock. Then he asked, "Why didn't you go through with it?"

"I don't believe in killing an innocent life. You have no room to pass judgment on Luke when you wanted me to kill this baby in the first place. So, shut up and leave us alone," I grumbled.

"I can't believe that you're sticking up for this psycho. He nearly killed you, Katrina, the baby, and your friends with the van. You're just as psychotic as he is, and you both need some serious help," he retorted loudly.

"No, I think that you're the one who is crazy and needs to get help. I think there's a mental unit, somewhere in this hospital," I declared.

"Please, calm down," Luke said, holding my hand.

"I'm sorry, it's just that he's making me so infuriated," I sighed.

"That's what he wants, so ignore him."

"Miss, I need to know if you are going to be pressing any charges," the officer stated.

"No, I'm not going to have the man I have idolized for most of my life arrested. But you can escort this slime ball out of my room," I told the cop, pointing to Mitch.

"I guess that I should leave, as well," Luke uttered, getting up.

"No, please stay here with me. I need you to hold me," I said, grabbing his arm.

"How can you want me here after what happened?" he questioned, looking puzzled.

"It was an accident, that's all," I told him.

"No, it wasn't," he replied.

"What are you saying?"

"I'm saying that I got drunk, got behind the wheel, went chasing after you guys, and hit the van. Please, believe me when I say that I didn't intend for it turn out the way that it did," Luke pleaded.

"I do believe you, and I forgive you. Now we share a common experience with alcohol. It will, however, take me a while before I can forget," I told him, trying to pull him closer.

"I don't deserve to even know you," he said, taking my hands off him.

"Please, Luke, just hold me for a few minutes," I pleaded.

"Just for a few minutes, then I need to go."

I pulled him down on the bed, put my arms around him, and snuggled up to him. He lowered his head and kissed my forehead. We sat there holding each other for a few minutes, and then he stood up.

"I'll be right back. I need to get some coffee."

"Okay. I'll miss you," I smiled.

"Ditto," he smiled back and then walked out.

A few minutes later, Jimmy and the cop came in. I told them that it was a mistake and not to pursue it any longer.

"Why aren't you pressing charges?" Jimmy asked.

"I can't explain it right now. If your brother wants to, I can't stop him. Just tell him to talk to Luke, and I'm sure that they can work something out," I explained as the cop left.

"When is he coming back?" Jimmy asked.

"He just went for some coffee."

"If he was going for coffee, he must've gone to a coffee shop," he responded.

"Why do you say that?"

"Because I saw him and his friends go outside."

"He told me that he would be right back," I cried.

"Maybe he will, I don't know," he said, shrugging his shoulders.

"I hope so; I really need him here with me," I sighed.

"My brother and I are heading back to Rhode Island soon. Maybe, when you get back, we can get together sometime," he stated.

"Sounds good, I'll look you up. Thanks for stopping by," I replied as I gave him a quick hug.

"Not a problem. Goodbye," he responded, and then strolled across the room and out the door.

The next couple of days it was the same old hospital routine; meals, visitors, tests, needles, etc.... On the third day of my stay, the doctor came in my room and told me that I could go home in a day or two. On the day that I was supposed to go home, I was told that I had to stay a couple of extra days. Then I found out from Katrina that the Falcons were over in Michigan somewhere. I took more tests in the next couple of days than I ever did in school. At suppertime, a nurse came in looking very pale and sad.

"What's wrong?" I asked her. "You look like someone at a funeral for a loved one."

"I'm sorry that I have to tell you this, but your baby died

last night," she regretfully replied.

My heart sank to my belly, tears filled my eyes, and my heart was racing. This couldn't be true. I don't remember any operation or anything.

"How can this be?" I moaned.

"The baby just couldn't hold on any longer in the state that it was in," she answered.

"What are you talking about? When? How? Why?" I blubbered.

"Calm down, Miss. You'll end up hyperventilating and then you'll be in worse shape. I will answer your questions as soon as you relax. In fact, I will give you a mild sedative to relax you a bit," she said as she reached for a needle on the table next to my bed.

At first, when she stuck the needle in my arm, it pinched a little. However, taking the needle back out seemed to hurt more. My arm twinged, and I screamed at her.

"Feeling better, now?" the nurse asked me a few minutes after she had administered the sedative into my arm.

"Yes, a little better," I whispered, feeling groggy all of a sudden.

"Good. Your baby's death was due to high alcohol in your bloodstream. Last night, you became unconscious in your sleep, so we checked your blood work and your other tests. That's when we noticed how high your blood-alcohol level was. We knew that we had to operate quickly. The doctors and other nurses tried very hard to save the baby, but there was just too much alcohol in the blood," she explained softly.

"No! This can't be! You're lying! Get out of here!" I screamed.

She didn't hesitate a bit, just turned around and left. I couldn't believe and didn't want to believe her. *How could the baby die from the alcohol and not from the accident?* I thought to myself. I felt like ending it all; my life was too messed up, and I couldn't handle it anymore. After a while, I ended up crying myself to sleep.

The next morning was like déjà vu. I woke up, and I didn't know where I was or how I got there. I called the nurse, she came in, and I asked her what had happened.

"You tried jumping out of the window in your sleep last night. We had to bring you to ICU and put you in a room that would be safe," she answered.

"Can I still go home?" I questioned.

"Yes, but you are required to see a therapist at least twice a week. You also need to call every day for a while, so the doctor knows your okay," she replied.

"I can do that, no problem."

About a half-hour later, my grandma came to take me home. She helped me pack my things, fill out the necessary paper work, and then wheeled me out to the car. I was very surprised that my grandmother didn't lecture me or ask any questions on the ride home. Maybe she found out about the suicide attempt and didn't want to upset me. When we reached the house, she carried my things into my room for me. Then she told me to lie down on the sofa while she made us some tea. A few minutes later, the kettle began whistling. She brought the tea into the parlor, sat down next to me on the sofa, and told me that we needed to talk.

"Gram, before you say anything. I want you to know that I know the mistakes that I've been making, and I've already decided how to start fixing things," I informed her.

"I am glad to hear all of that, but you don't realize the scare that you gave me and the rest of your family," she cried.

"I know, and I am sorry. But I also know that it's not good enough to be sorry, and that's why I've decided to still get help when I return to Rhode Island."

"I am happy that you said that, because I was going to tell you to do that. I was afraid that you might resent me if I told you that."

"Just to let you know, I wouldn't have felt like that. I love you too much to resent you," I responded, hugging her.

"Thank you, dear. That means a lot to me."

"I hate to cut this short, but I'm feeling tired," I yawned.

"That's okay; you go on up to bed and get some rest. I'll see you in the morning," she assured me, helping me off the sofa.

I didn't even bother to undress; I just hopped into bed and fell fast asleep.

The next morning was bright and warm. The sun's rays warmed my skin as I crept out of bed. It was the perfect day for a jog, but my body wasn't ready for that yet. When I had finished my eggs and toast, my gram suggested that we go to Katrina's house for a while. I didn't ask any questions or argue with her, I wanted to go. As soon as we got in the door to Katrina's house, Mother Nature started calling me. While I went to answer the call, my gram went in the den to talk with Katrina's mom. When I was done, I walked into the den and immediately the room became silent.

"Did I interrupt something?" I asked them, looking around the room.

"No," Katrina's mom replied.

"What gave you that idea?" Gram asked, turning her face away.

"It got quiet when I walked in. Plus, you two look very suspicious," I answered, not believing their answers.

"We were just talking about that group that you girls had gone to see," Gram smiled.

"Oh, I see," I said. I did believe that, for some reason.

We left Katrina's, shortly after that. The next few days were about the same. I woke up, ate, slept, woke up again, ate a little more, and then went to bed until the following day and started all over again.

On the fourth day of my recovery, I had a visitor. Katrina came over around noon to spend some time with me and have some lunch. After we were done eating, we took a short walk around the block.

"So, what are you going to do when you get back to Rhode Island?" she asked as we stopped to rest under a tree.

"What do you mean?" I asked her.

"I mean with your life. Like a job or school," she implied politely.

"I'll probably stay with my mom at first. After I have saved enough, I'll get my own place. I still have some of the money leftover that I'd found on the beach, but it's not enough for an apartment down there. I might go to college part-time so I can still get a job," I explained.

"Are you still going to take psychology and all of the courses that you had told me about before?" she questioned.

"I still might, but not in college."

"You are going to be very busy with all of your courses and a job," she said.

"Hopefully some of the courses won't be everyday. If they are, then I'll have no social life for a while."

"I think that I will go to law school. I just need to figure out which one," Katrina told me.

"Good for you!" I exclaimed, patting her back. "Are you going to wait for Cody until you go to school?"

"No, I don't think so."

"Why is that?"

"It's over between us. He left without saying goodbye or anything."

"You don't mean that, I know you don't," I said, trying to reason with her.

"Yes, I do. Just leave me alone," she cried, running away.

I tried calling out to her, but she kept on running. It upset me the way she left, but I knew that she would cool off eventually. When she did, I would be there for her.

When I arrived home, my grandma told me that a young man called while I was out.

"Was it Luke?" I asked her, elated at the very idea that it could've been him.

"No, it was a guy named Jimmy. He said that he would try again later. Sorry, dear," she answered, noticing the frown forming on my face.

"Oh, that's okay. It was stupid of me to get excited before I knew for sure," I sighed.

Tired from my walk, I went upstairs and took a nap. Not too much time had past when a loud ringing awoken me. Then I heard Gram tell me to pick the telephone up.

"Hello," I said.

"Hi, Vicki. It's me, Jimmy," he replied.

"What's up?" I asked him.

"Not too much. I just called to tell you that my brother got his van back, and I have a few items here for you and Katrina," he stated.

"How did you get the van back?" I inquired curiously. "I thought it was totaled."

"It was, but your friend Luke gave my brother enough money to get it fixed," he answered.

"That was nice of him to send John the money," I uttered.

"He didn't send it. He gave him a blank check at the hospital that same night. I thought you already knew that."

"No, I didn't. I haven't seen him since that night."

"Oh, I see. Anyway, he gave me a couple of things to give to you and Katrina," Jimmy said.

"If you want, you can bring them by tomorrow," I suggested.

"Sure, I can do that. I'll probably come by around 4:30," he responded.

"I am going to Katrina's in the afternoon, so just go there," I told him.

"Okay, but I need directions," he replied.

"That's right, I forgot. She lives in a big white farm house that sits next to a white church, off Main Street," I informed him.

"It sounds easy enough to find. I'm a little familiar with the area, but if I do get lost, I'll be sure to call."

"Well, I guess I will see you tomorrow," I replied.

"All right then, see ya," he said, and then hung up.

I tried to call Katrina, but no one answered the telephone.

So I got up and went downstairs. There was a note on the kitchen table from my grandmother telling me that she would be back soon. After I made myself a sandwich and took it into the living room, someone knocked on the door. I stood up, walked over to the door, and opened it.

"What do you want?" I posed, seeing Mitch standing there.

"Is that any way to greet a loved one?" he asked me, pushing his way past me and into the house.

"No, but it is the way to treat scum like you. Especially, when you just barge in like that," I stated.

"I'm sorry about that; I just wanted to make sure that I could talk to you," he responded.

"Begging and pleading would have been a nicer approach," I snickered, sitting down at the kitchen table.

"I'm not like that, sorry," he sneered, walking up to the table.

"So, why are you here?" I questioned.

"Because I care about you, and I wanted to see how you and the baby were doing," Mitch answered, sitting down next to me.

"Like you really care."

"I do."

"For your information, there is no baby."

"What do you mean, 'there is no baby'?" he questioned loudly.

"The baby died of alcohol poisoning," I mumbled, feeling my eyes fill with tears.

"You mean to tell me that you killed the baby," he retorted, and then looked around, as if he was thinking about something.

"What are you thinking, Mitch?"

"That you are a murderous, psychotic, and ruthless person," he remarked, and then added as he slapped me across the face, "I just can't believe you."

At first, I was in total shock. Then the pain in my face dominated me. It guided me to voice my response to his actions, "How dare you hit me! Get out of here!"

"Fine, I will. I can't stand to be around you anyway," he snapped as he stood up.

"Before you go, I just wanted to tell you something," I said, grabbing his arm.

"What's that?" he asked.

"That you're a fine one to be passing judgment when you wanted me to kill the baby in the first place."

"That was then," he snapped.

"You're such a hypocritical, son of a sea witch," I sneered.

"Whatever, I'm out of here," he replied, briskly walking over to the opened door and slamming it behind him.

Just then, the telephone started ringing. I quickly stood up, ran to the parlor, and picked it up on the fourth ring.

"Hello," I panted.

"Vicki, it's Katrina," she called out.

"Hi, Katrina," I said.

"What's wrong, you sound out of breath?"

"Mitch and I just had a fight, and then I ran to answer the phone," I answered.

"Why were you two fighting?"

"We were fighting because the miscarriage."

"Oh, I see. My mom told me about what happened, and she found out from your grandmother. I am very sorry that you had to go through that."

"Thanks, Katrina. I'll get over it, someday."

"The reason for my call is to apologize for the way I've been acting," she conveyed.

"That's okay, I understand. I do have some good news for you about Cody," I told her.

"You do!" she shrieked, her voice penetrated my eardrums.

"Yes, Luke gave that guy Jimmy a couple of things for you and me. He's bringing them by your place tomorrow," I explained.

"Cool, I can't wait to see what it is," she cried happily.

We kept talking until our ears felt like cauliflower, then we hung up and I went to bed.

I woke up late the next day, so I raced downstairs, ate a quick snack, showered, threw my clothes on, and took my Gram's car to Katrina's. It was about 3:00 p.m. when I arrived at her house, so I still had some time before Jimmy showed up. Katrina and I were both anxious and excited about the items that Jimmy was bringing us. Her mom suggested taking a walk to calm our nerves. We walked down the road for a little while, then turned around and headed back to her house. Jimmy was waiting outside her door when we arrived. He told us that he had just pulled in the driveway a few seconds ago, so we shouldn't worry about him having to wait or anything.

"I can't stay long; I just wanted to drop off the stuff for you girls," he said, walking to his car.

"We really appreciate you doing this for us," I told him as I followed him over.

"Yes, we sure do," Katrina smiled.

- 6 -
The Surprise

"It's no problem, I'm glad to do it," he replied as he reached for a paper bag sitting on the front seat.

"Thank you, sir," I replied while he handed the bag to me.

"You're very welcome. I'd like to stay and chat, but I must be hitting the road. I'll call you sometime soon," Jimmy said, getting in the car.

"Okay, thanks again," I said waving to him as he pulled out of the driveway.

Excited, Katrina grabbed the bag from me and reached inside. She pulled out two envelopes and two music boxes, both with our names on them. Katrina opened the envelope and found a letter from Cody. It read:

My dearest Katrina,

The reason I left the way that I did was the accident. I feel partly responsible, I could've prevented it, and I didn't. There was a lot of anger and jealousy inside of me. I had no control of any of my emotions. I know that's no excuse, but it's the truth. Someday, I hope that you can find it in your heart and mind to forgive me. I miss you very much. We should be back in Maine in a few months. Maybe then we can sit down and talk about things, like us. Tell Vicki I said hello. How is she? She's probably, about the same as Luke. He's been going up the walls since the accident. We've tried everything, but nothing seems to work. I hope that you are having better luck with Vicki. I have to go now, but I will be in touch real soon.

Love ya lots & Miss ya,
Cody

After she finished reading, she began weeping and laughing. I figured that her letter had to have been amusing. Then I proceeded to read the letter from my envelope. It read:

My sweet Vicki,

I don't know where to begin. I guess I will start by apologizing for what happened. You almost lost your life and the life of your baby because of me. Then I lied to you and left you when you needed me the most. Don't feel guilty about the hatred that you must have for me. I don't blame you if you never want anything to do with me ever again. Please believe me when I say how truly sorry I am and that I do care deeply for you. Maybe this letter and gift aren't much, but for now, I hope that they will do. I swear to you, that until I die, I will continue to try to make up for what I did. There is so much fear and confusion inside of me, but I have to shape up for the concert and for the band. I love you and I hope that you already knew that. If you didn't, you do now. Take care of yourself.

Love always,
Luke

P.S. I'll always be there for you when you need me. Just search your heart, and you'll find me.

I didn't laugh, but I did cry when I had finished reading it. The song from the music box reminded me of a ballet that I had seen when I was a little girl. It was a sad ballet, and at the time, I didn't quite understand it. Now I could almost relate to the heroine in the story. The sadness was overwhelming, and I wanted to be gone. There was only one safe way to do it, go to sleep. I drove home and went straight to bed.

The next morning was hectic and confusing. Everyone was calling and telling my brother and me to come up to the beach one last time. We were leaving soon, and they wanted to hang out for old time's sake.

My brother and I got ready and then left for the beach. As soon as we arrived, everybody came up to us and handed out their addresses. When the chaos ended, we all went swimming and played "King or Queen of the Lake." After a couple of hours, they started to leave. They all said that they had places to be, so we didn't argue.

Since everyone had left, we decided to go back home. When we got home, we went inside; I noticed that the lights were off and that it was very quiet. Thinking that Gram had stepped out for a bit, I turned the lights on. The next thing I knew; people were popping out and yelling, "Surprise!" You can imagine the shock that we experienced when they did that. I peered into the parlor, and noticed that it had been decorated much like the kitchen. There were flowers, balloons, streamers, stringed lights, and centerpieces throughout both rooms. They took us out back where there were more decorations, tables, chairs, and a buffet spread out along two long tables. The patio was empty and I didn't know why.

"Gram, why is the patio empty?" I asked her.

"No particular reason. It just worked out like that," she replied.

"Thank you for the party. It's just what I needed," I said as I embraced her.

"You're welcome," she said, patting my back.

Katrina took me upstairs so that I could change into something more comfortable. When I was finished, we headed back to the party. I wasn't wearing anything spectacular, just a white jumpsuit, a light pink blouse, a belt to match the shirt, and white tennis sneakers. As we were coming out the back door that led to the patio, two hands went over our eyes. Then a pair of hands led us (I assumed at the time) outside and sat us down on a couple of chairs.

"What's going on?" I asked whoever was around.

"It's a surprise, Vicki. You'll find out soon enough," a voice replied that sounded like my brother, Matt.

A few minutes later, the hands left our eyes, and we could see. That's when I saw instruments a few feet in front of me, and then I looked up and saw the Falcons coming around the corner of the house. Everyone began clapping, cheering, and taking pictures of Katrina's face and mine. I don't know about Katrina, but I was definitely in shock. We looked at each other, shrugged our shoulders, and looked away with our noses turned up. They came up to us and shook our hands, then went over to their instruments. Looking around at everyone, I noticed their eyes bulging and their mouths dropped. Obviously they were surprised at our reaction to the band.

"What is wrong with you two girls?" my grandmother asked us as she approached us.

"Nothing is wrong," I answered.

"If nothing was wrong, you would've seemed a bit happier about your surprise guests," Katrina's mom said to us.

"It's a long and sad story, Mom. You wouldn't understand even if we were to tell you. Which, as far as I know, we are not going to do. I don't mean to sound rude, it's just difficult to talk about, okay?" Katrina informed her mother.

"I am sorry to hear that, if we had known—" Gram started to say, but I interrupted her.

"It's okay, don't fret. It's still a nice surprise," I told her as they returned to their seats.

"This first song is called, 'Love is a Reason to Live.' We would like to dedicate it to a couple of special friends of ours," Luke told everyone.

It was a pretty song, but kind of sad, too. Most of the words seemed to be about the suicide death of a young girl who had been in love with the wrong man.

"How would they like it if we embarrassed them like this?" Katrina asked as she was laughing.

Luke continued to sing until Matthew went up to him and whispered something. Then Warren and Mitch picked us up off the chairs and carried us to the patio. We put up a good fight, but it didn't us any good.

"Did you girls say that you wanted to do the same thing to us?" Luke asked us, smiling.

"That's right," I answered.

"But, we were only joking," Katrina replied.

"Come on, let's really do it," I whispered to her.

"Are you serious?" she asked me, putting her hands on her hips.

"We're dead serious. In fact, I have the perfect music," I told her as I motioned her to follow me into the shed.

"Okay," Katrina said, following me.

"We'll do three songs, 'It Should Be Me,' 'Time to Change,' and 'Who Knows What Love Is." You do know the words and music for these songs, right?" I asked

"Right, but I only know how to play the keyboard. We'll have to find a couple of people to play the drums and guitar," she told me.

"Go get Mark and Tony; I heard that they could play pretty good music," I told Katrina, and she walked over to the buffet tables to get them.

Then I went over to Luke and told him to go sit down with everyone else. While we were setting up, everybody returned to his or her seats to wait.

"The first song that we would like to play for you is an oldie but a real goodie. It's called, 'It Should Be Me,'" I told everyone as we started to play the music.

It was a short but very sweet song, and everyone seemed to love it. They were on their feet, cheering, whistling, clapping, hooting, and hollering.

"The next song will be a duet between Katrina and I. We want to dedicate it to the special people in our lives this summer. When this song is over, we're going to go right on to the next and final one. The last song is called, 'Who Knows What Love Is,'" I explained to our audience.

"Vicki, you forgot to tell them the name of the duet that we're doing," Katrina reminded me.

"Oh, I guess I did. Sorry, it's called, 'Time to Change.'"

Everybody began clapping as Katrina walked up next to me with her microphone. I didn't realize until now how beautiful her voice really was. After we were done with songs, we received the same reaction from the audience as before. So we all bowed, said thanks, then Luke came up to hug me, but I backed away.

"What's wrong? I thought that you wanted to see me."

"I did, but I guess you didn't really listen to the second song we sang," I replied.

"Oh, Vicki, come here and give me a nice, warm hug," Mitch said to me as he approached my side.

"I don't believe this. Neither one of you were even listening," I cried, running away from them and into the house. Mitch followed me into the house, and then Luke came in after him.

"Mitch, please get rid of him. I don't want to see him," I sobbed.

"I just want to talk with you for a minute," Luke said to me.

"Forget it! When I needed someone to talk to, you weren't there. You not only lied to me, you also abandoned me," I told him, still crying.

"But I can explain everything," he replied.

"I don't care if you can; I want you out of here, now. In fact, I want both of you to leave. I hate you both, and I never want to see either of you ever again," I yelled as I ran away.

I heard footsteps from behind me, and they were getting closer. As I turned to see who it was, from out of nowhere, a set of lips touched mine. So, I pushed the person away from me, opened my eyes, and saw Luke standing in front of me.

"I thought that I had made it clear to you that I wanted nothing to do with you, ever!" I yelled, trying to walk past him.

"Please, just hear me out," he pleaded, reaching for my arm.

"Let me go, you barbaric a**!" I told him, slapping him across the face.

"Fine, if that's what you want," Luke uttered, walking away with his head facing down.

Cody, Katrina, David, and Simon walked up to me and begged me to give Luke just five minutes to say his piece. After a few minutes of begging and pleading, I finally gave in. I knew that if I hadn't, they never would have left me alone. They told me that he was in the front yard, so I went out there.

"Luke, I want to apologize for hitting you. What I am trying to say is that I could've handled it better. To atone for my actions, I will grant you five minutes to make your peace," I explained to him.

"Thank you, but you didn't need to apologize. I deserved what I got and more," he replied. "I meant everything that I said in the letter. I will make up for everything that I have done to you and your baby for as long as I live."

"There's something that you need to know," I uttered.

"What's that?" he asked.

"The baby died from alcohol poisoning, not from the accident. So there's nothing to make up for," I replied, looking away.

"Oh, I see. I don't know what to say, other than I am truly sorry," Luke said, moving his hand across my back.

"Your five minutes is up, now. Was there anything else that you wanted to say?"

"Only that I do care about you, and to ask for your forgiveness. If it's possible, I would like for us to remain friends," he told me.

"That sounds good to me," I said.

"If you want, I'll stop by before you leave," Luke hinted to me.

"I've decided to leave tomorrow, so do what you want. I really don't care one way or the other."

"What's wrong with you? I was under the impression that you had forgiven me."

"I have, it's just that I'm exhausted. I'll see you tomorrow, if you come by," I told him as I walked back into the house.

A few minutes later, Katrina walked into the parlor, where I was sitting. She informed me that everyone had left, and she wanted to find out what happened between Luke and me.

"Not too much. He just blubbered out a bunch of stuff, I forgave him, and that was it," I explained.

"Then what's wrong?" she asked.

"I guess that I can't lie to you, you always see right through me. I waited and waited for him to tell me that he loved me like he did in the letter, but he didn't," I cried softly.

"Maybe he felt that he didn't have enough time," she suggested.

"B*@+#%, he only wrote what he wrote to compensate for his guilt. Now that he knows that he has my forgiveness, he doesn't find it necessary to lie to me," I told her.

"Do you honestly believe that?" Katrina asked, looking down at me.

"Yep, because if he really did love me, those would have been the first words out of his mouth."

"I don't know what else to say. You seem totally convinced in your beliefs," Katrina said.

"That's okay."

"I hate to cut this short, but Cody is waiting outside for me. We're going for a ride to talk and anything else that comes up."

"It's all right, I'm feeling a bit tired anyway," I responded.

"Are you sure?" she asked.

"Positive. Now get out of here and have some fun. I'll see you tomorrow before I leave," I answered.

"Where are you going?"

"I've decided to leave tomorrow instead of in a couple of days. I'm sorry, I forgot to tell you."

"I wish that you would stay a little longer, but I do understand your desire to leave sooner."

"Thank you, I really needed to hear that. Now go, before we keep on gabbing," I chuckled, motioning for her to go.

"I'm going already. Call me before you leave so we can say goodbye and all of that other stuff that you do when someone leaves," she said, walking out the door.

After staring out the window and daydreaming, I drifted off to sleep in the armchair.

Morning came, and I was up at the rooster's crow. This day started out quite hectic, like the day before. There was so much to pack and little time to do it in. I wanted to be on the road by noon so that I could avoid rush-hour traffic in Boston. I still had to eat, shower, get dressed, and go get my car from Daniel's house. When all of that was done, my brother and I packed up the car, then went back inside and packed some snacks for the road. As I was putting ice in the cooler, there was a knock on the door. Expecting it to be Luke, I rushed to the door and opened it. To my disappointment, it wasn't Luke. It was Katrina and the other members of the band. They motioned me to come outside with them, so I did.

"You know what; I was ready to apologize to that moron for the way that I acted yesterday. Since he decided not to show up, I guess that I can't," I snapped, pacing the driveway.

"He was going to show up, but he figured that you were

still mad at him. He gave me these to give to you, instead," Cody replied, handing me a dozen red roses and an autographed picture of Luke.

"Just like at the hospital, he lies and never says goodbye. He thinks that he can buy me. Well, forget it!" I shouted as I threw the gifts on the ground.

"We tried to convince him to come, but he wouldn't," David explained.

"Yeah, we're really sorry about this," Simon expressed.

"He did say that he loved you, but only as a friend," Cody remarked.

"Love, uh. Luke doesn't even know the meaning of love," I retorted.

"We can't stay long, we wanted to come by to say farewell, give you the gifts, and wish you the best of luck," David said.

"Yeah, thanks for stopping by and everything. If you can, call me sometime or write to me," I told them as I wrote down my mom's telephone number and address.

"We will. So long," Simon replied, shaking my hand.

"See you soon. If you can, try to come to our concerts, when we're in town," Cody said to me as he hugged me.

"Bye, Vicki," David called out from the car.

"Bye, guys!" I yelled, as they backed out of the driveway.

"I guess this is goodbye, Katrina. I am going to miss you so much," I cried as we embraced for the last time.

"I will miss you, too," Katrina cried.

"Promise me that you will keep in touch," I told her.

"I will, if you will," she replied.

"I definitely will," I stated.

"Well, I better get going. They might take off without me," she remarked, pointing to their car sitting at the edge of the driveway near the road.

"Okay, see you around," I said as she slowly walked towards their car.

When they left, I ran back into the house with tears dripping down my face. Just as I entered the bathroom, the telephone rang. I went to answer it, but my brother beat me to it, and I went back into the bathroom. After I blew my nose and wiped my face, I went out to the kitchen and finished packing up the cooler.

"Who was on the phone, Matt?" I asked my brother.

7
Rhode Island

"It was one of my friends from the beach. He was calling to say goodbye," Matt replied.

"Oh," I said, walking around to make sure that I had everything packed up.

About an hour later, we were ready to hit the road. We said goodbye to our grandmother. Thanked her for everything that she did for us, and told her that we would call her as soon as we arrived safely home. Matt and I didn't say much to each other when we first set out on our journey. About an hour or two later, he spoke up and told me that he needed something to drink. I stopped at a gas station off one of the exits so he could get some beverages for us. He walked in the store, while I put more gas in my car.

Mother Nature started calling after I was done pumping the gas. I walked over to the restrooms and went in. When I had finished, I opened the stall door and saw someone in a ski mask coming at me. I tried to fend the offender off, but I couldn't. A smelly cloth was placed over my mouth and I was held me very tightly. It started to get very dark around me, and I felt faint.

When I opened my eyes, I saw that I was no longer in the restroom, but in a motel room. It was small, stinky, and very shabby. That's when I figured out that someone must've kidnapped me. Who was it, and why? *Matt must be worried sick about me,* I thought to myself. I looked around the best that I could, trying to find any clues as to where I was and who had kidnapped me. All I found was a note on a small nightstand near the only door. I walked over to the night stand, picked up the note, and began to read it. It read:

To whom it may concern,

I do not wish to harm you in any way or plan on it. The only reason that you are here is so that we can communicate. I will release you tonight. Please, don't be afraid or worried. You are safe and close to home.

Anonymous

That's what all kidnappers say, what a line of horse poo, I thought.

About fifteen minutes later, the door opened and in walked the person in the ski mask. Now that I had a better look at the person, I could tell by the walk and build that it was a man. He was carrying two plastic bags of groceries and a funny looking device.

"I'm glad to see that you're awake, because I bought us some food," he said, setting the bags on the table next to the bed.

His voice seemed odd; it was a little raspy and wavered through my body. I could feel the hair on my arms stand up and the goose bumps that were forming there.

"I am sort of hungry. Being kidnapped kind of brings the hunger out in me. There are a couple of things that you need to be aware of," I told him.

"What's that?" he asked.

"For one, I don't believe all of that horse poo in your little note to me. Secondly, I have questions for you, and I expect answers to all of them. Finally, don't think for one moment that you scare me, because you don't."

"It's all true; I don't wish to harm you. All that I want to do is talk. I'm glad that you are not afraid, because there is nothing to fear. After we eat, you may ask your questions," he replied.

So we sat down at the table, ate our subs, chips, and salads, and drank our soda pop. By the time we were finished, I was feeling a bit tired and decided to start asking my questions.

"I have a list of questions, so be prepared," I told him.

"I'm ready, go ahead and ask away," he said, reclining back in his chair.

"Here it goes: What is your purpose with me? What is the date and time? Did you orchestrate this thing, or was it done on a whim? Was this planned? How and why me? Where are we? Who are you?" I asked.

"I told you that you were here so that we could talk. It's the same day that you left Maine, it's about 6:15 p.m., and you are close to home," he responded.

"What about answers to my others questions, and what could we possibly have to talk about?" I inquired.

"That's all I am going to say for now," he remarked as he got up and walked away.

"If you don't answer the rest of my questions, then I will scream really loud, and the cops will come."

"If you try, I will have to put a gag in your mouth, and I really don't want to," he said softly.

"You wouldn't be able to if I kept my mouth shut. This means that you would have to pry it open, and that means hurting me. You've already told me that you wouldn't do that. I guess your only option is to answer my questions," I explained.

He started to move towards me, but he didn't get too close because I kicked him hard in the groin. Then I proceeded to wrap my legs around his head, when he bent over in pain, and pulled his mask off. Shocked at the face behind the mask, I released him and dropped to the floor.

"It's you, I don't believe this!" I shrieked. "How could you do this to me, Luke?" I posed, still in a state of shock.

"I am really sorry if I scared you or hurt you in any way. I felt it was the only way to get you to talk with me without walking away from me or hitting me," he replied, trying to stand up.

"I guess that you were wrong," I sneered, pointing to his groin.

"Yeah, I guess so," he said, still somewhat hunched over.

"Nevertheless, that is a lame excuse. Did it ever dawn on you that I could hate you afterwards?" I asked, getting up and walking over to the bed.

"No. It didn't really. I didn't care about the consequences. As long as I could straighten things out with you."

"There's nothing else that you want to say to me?" I hinted.

"No, should there be?" he questioned.

"I was just curious, that's all. Now if you don't mind, I'd like to leave."

"Not until we straighten things out," he stated.

"Well, at least come sit closer to me on the bed," I said to him as I slowly scooted towards the back of the bed.

"I guess that I can do that," he replied, walking over to the bed.

When he was close enough, I pulled him on top of me and began kissing him lavishly. I was surprised that he didn't pull away and that he was going along with it. Although it felt good to have him in my arms, to be kissing with him, I had to stop.

"Please stop and get off me," I beseeched him.

"Why, what's wrong? Don't you want to do this?" he questioned, appearing astonished at my plea.

"I only did this, to show you what it was like to have someone play head games with you," I told him, getting off the bed.

"I never did this to you," Luke remarked.

"Oh, yes, you did. You made me believe that you wanted me and you loved me," I stated.

"I never said or did anything to make you believe any of that," he replied.

"You told me that you loved me in the letter that you gave to Jimmy to give to me. Then at the park, you treated me like I was your lady," I cried.

"I do love you, but as a friend. I'm sorry if my words or actions misled you in some way," he expressed, putting his arm around my shoulders.

I pulled away and said to him, "You know what? You're just like Mitch. You're always sorry for something, and I am sorry that I ever met either of you," I sobbed.

"You don't really mean that," he said.

"Yes, I do. Just because you're a rock star, it doesn't mean that you're perfect. To me, you're another jack*** out for a little roll in the hay," I said, wiping away the tears.

"Now you're going too far. I'm—" he started saying, but I interrupted him.

"If you weren't a jack***, then you wouldn't have been kissing me the way you were," I informed him.

"I—" he started to say, but again I interrupted.

"I'm right, aren't I?"

"No. If you would let me say what I have to say, then you would see that I'm telling the truth," Luke replied. When he thought that it was still okay for him to speak, he said, "You don't understand. At first, that's all I wanted. But when I saw you at the concert, and the more that I got to know you, I wanted more," he explained.

"So I was right," I replied.

"No, just listen. After I knew you better, I realized that I had too much respect for you to use you. You've had enough problems in your life, and I didn't want to add any more. I wanted it to be right for both of us."

"Well, I guess that I owe you an apology for what I called you, and for what I said."

"You don't have to apologize. I understand," he sighed as he moved near me.

"Now that everything has been straightened out, I want to leave," I stated.

"Why?" he asked.

"You told me that you would release me when were done talking, and we're done."

"No, there is still more to be said," Luke said.

"Like what?"

"How do you feel about being lovers?" he questioned with a slight smile.

"There's nothing to say about it. I had a dream about being with you intimately, but it's gone."

"What do you mean by that?" he inquired.

"Don't worry about it; it's not even worth uttering."

"I see now; this is a guilt trip."

"No, it isn't. I just don't want to get into it," I told him.

"Well, I am giving you tonight to make up your mind about us," he told me, walking toward the sink.

"Your little statement is a joke. Let's just forget that we ever met. So, I guess there's your answer," I cackled, walking over to the window.

"No, I can't. I'm falling in love with you, and I don't know how to handle it," he remarked as he approached me.

"Join the Lonely Hearts Club, maybe they can help," I sneered.

"Don't be so snotty; I'm trying to tell you how I feel. I want to be with you, I've always wanted that. I guess, because of my ego, I didn't realize it soon enough," he replied softly.

"Better luck—" I began saying, but this time he stopped me.

"Vicki, please, just let me have tonight. Let me feel your warm, sensuous, body close to me. I want to love you heart and soul on our last night together," Luke expressed, pulling me to him as he pressed his lips against my neck.

"Oh, Luke, I want the same thing, but I don't want this to be our last night together. We can call each other and write, can't we?" I cried, turning to face him.

"Of course we can. As long as that is what you really want."

"Yes, I want us to always keep in touch," I replied.

"Does that mean you will be mine?"

"What do you mean by 'mine'?"

"My lover," he answered.

"But, for how long?" I questioned, drying my face with the sleeve of my shirt.

"I don't know; let's just take it one day at a time," he responded.

"I need to know before we go any further."

"Okay, it would be like we were dating, but nothing serious," he explained.

"Why wouldn't it be serious? If you are in love with me, then it would be?" I questioned, feeling a bit confused by what he said.

"Right now, I am still doing gigs at bars and concerts at different places, you're enrolling in college. I'd rather take you out a few times so that we can be better acquainted with one another. Who knows, we might not be made for one another," he explained.

"I can always go on the road with you, so that we can get to know each other more. College can wait until spring or even next fall."

"I can't let you do that. You might end up resenting yourself and me down the road sometime," Luke replied, caressing my back.

"It's my life, and I wouldn't resent either one of us. This is my chance for happiness, and I won't throw it away."

"Truth is, I would feel uncomfortable and tied down," he said.

"Oh, I see," I said, pulling away from his slight hold and walking towards the door.

"That's good, now let us try and get some sleep. We have a good ride ahead of us, so we need some rest," Luke suggested, heading over to the bed.

"Sounds good to me, I was feeling a bit tired," I replied, following him over.

"Are you sure that everything is okay?" he asked.

"Yep, I'm sure," I answered, but thought the opposite.

"If you want, I'll sleep on the chair and you can have the bed."

"No, I don't mind sharing the bed with you," I told him politely.

"If that's what you want, but I'm not ready for bed yet," Luke replied.

"Okay, goodnight," I said, looking at him seductively.

"Goodnight, and sleep well," he whispered, moving closer to me.

I walked over to my side of the bed and slowly got into bed while he watched. After a few minutes had passed, Luke came to bed.

I turned to him and asked, "Would you do me a small favor?"

"Sure. Just name it and it's yours," he answered.

"Would you hold me for a few minutes?" I inquired.

"Yes, but I thought that you were tired."

"I am tired. I just want to feel your arms around me one last time," I told him.

As he scooted closer to me, he asked, "What's the real reason for this? Because you should already know that this won't be the last time. I don't plan on leaving for a couple of days."

"All right, you caught me. The real reason is because I'm a little cold, and I thought that you would think that I was being silly."

"No, I wouldn't have, and I don't. It is a bit chilly in here, and even though there are blankets, I will still hold you."

I sat up in bed while he moved in behind me. Then I nestled up to him, he wrapped his arms around me, and we just sat there quiet and still. All of a sudden, he began gently squeezing me and sliding his hands up and down my arms.

"Are you cold still?" he inquired.

"Yes, just a bit."

"I'll pull the blankets up more, that way we will be nice and toasty," he whispered to me as he pulled the comforter and afghan on us.

Then he brushed his face in my hair, and began working down my neck. His mouth pressed softly along the lining of my neck, and across my shoulders. My blood was boiling, my entire body was burning from his love kisses, but I had to control him and myself.

"Luke," I whispered.

"Yes?" he softly replied while kissing my shoulders.

"Could you please stop?" I murmured.

"Why? Don't you want this?" he questioned, still kissing my upper body.

"I do, but not like this. As you said earlier, I want this to be the right time for both of us. This would feel like a one-night stand to me," I responded.

"It's not going to be like that," he remarked as we both sat up more.

"You're going to be on the road a lot, and you made it seem like you didn't want me tagging along. I don't want to feel like I'm at your beck and call," I told him, sliding over to the edge of the bed.

"I have already told you that it wouldn't be like that. I wish that you would believe me," Luke expressed, sliding up next to me.

"It's going to take some time before that will happen. Right now, all I want to do is sleep. It's been a long and tiring day," I told him as I moved back to my side of the bed and got under the covers.

"Okay, goodnight and sweet dreams," he replied, leaning over and kissing my forehead.

A SUMMER AFFAIR

I knew that I wasn't going to have a good night until I got out of there and was home. As soon as it got late enough to where I knew that he was sound asleep, I got up, wrote a note to him, and left it on the night stand. The note said:

Dear Luke,

By the time you read this, I will be either home or close to it. I can't have things the way that you want them to be. I need a relationship. It's time for me to settle down and start doing something with my life. I can't just see you whenever it's convenient for you or just talk on the telephone unless there is a commitment between us. It is a known fact, no rock musician can settle down with just one woman. We're just not meant to be!

Love always,
Vicki

P.S. Thanks for everything. Remember that we will always be friends, so keep in touch.

- 8 -
Runaway

When I was done reading it over to make sure that I hadn't forgotten anything, I looked over at Luke in the bed and then left. I walked over to the office and asked the manager where I was, what time it was, and where I could find the nearest payphone. Looking at me a bit odd, he told me in a low voice that I was in Freetown, Massachusetts, that it was 3:00 a.m., and that I could use his telephone. I called my mom's house to see if Matt was there and could come get me. It rang a few times before someone finally answered.

"Hello," a female voice whispered.

"Mom, I'm sorry that I woke you up, but I need to know if Matt is there," I replied.

"No, I was under the impression that you two were together," she remarked in a slightly panicked tone.

"We were, but I'll explain it to you when I get there. I'm sure Matt is okay and with friends. I love you, Mom."

"Okay, I'll see you when you get here. I love you, too," she replied, and then hung up.

I thanked the man for letting me use the telephone and then headed towards the highway to try to hitch a ride. There weren't many vehicles out on the road, which meant that it was going to be hard to catch a ride. About a few miles down the road, a tractor-trailer pulled off and picked me up. The man appeared to be in his mid to late forties. He had long gray hair, a white moustache and beard, a round and slightly large body, and a cheery smile. In some weird but merry way, he reminded me of St. Nick, which made me feel safe.

He offered me some of his hot cocoa and cookies, and then allowed me to hop in the back where he sleeps and get some rest. I thanked him for his generosity and kindness. I fell asleep quickly. It was bright and sunny when I awoke, and we had pulled off the highway. The trucker told me that we were in Fall River, and this was as far he was going. I thanked him again, and he wished me luck and a safe journey. He had dropped me off near a mall that I was familiar with, so I knew which way to go. I got back on the highway and began heading east when I noticed a black mustang coming towards me. The car pulled off the road in front of me and stopped. I saw that the license plates were from Maine. It looked just like my car, so I figured it was Matt. I quickly ran up to the car and got in.

"What in the world happened to you?" I asked him as pulled back on the highway.

"What do you mean?" Matt inquired.

"Where were you when I was being held prisoner by some crazed madman?" I posed.

"Give me a break. You were not being held by a crazy person, and you know it," he sneered.

"So, you were in it on with him, weren't you?" I questioned.

"Yes. Luke filled me in on his plan back in Maine. I thought that it might work, so I agreed to help him."

"Well, it didn't. It made things worse, but I don't blame you for that. It's his fault that this has ended this way."

"I am sorry it didn't work out."

"Don't be, it just wasn't meant to be."

After that was said, we didn't talk too much for the rest of the trip. As soon as we arrived home, I grabbed my stuff from the trunk, went upstairs, and went to bed. Later that day, I woke up and felt like going to the beach. My brother told me that he'd meet me there in a little while, so I headed out. When I arrived at the beach, I found a parking spot and a place to sit close to the snack bar where I met up with a friend of mine.

"Hi, Marly," I said as she approached me. "What have you been up to?"

"Hi, Vicki. It's been so long since we last saw each other. I think about three or four months? I haven't really been doing much; my summer was a bore," Marly answered cheerfully, embracing me.

"Sorry to hear that, but my summer wasn't any better. I can't say that it was boring; it was just a complete disaster."

"I'm sorry. What happened?" she asked as I was rung up at the snack bar.

"Thank you, have a nice day," I told the cashier as she handed me my soda. "Sorry about that. Now, I'll try to answer your question as briefly as I can. I was knocked up, beat up, had two boyfriends, got intoxicated, had a blackout, met the Falcons, was in a car accident, had a miscarriage due to alcohol poisoning, broke up with both boyfriends, was kidnapped by Luke Nash, turned him down and left him…and that's about it," I explained quickly, trying to catch my breath.

"Oh my goodness! I guess you weren't kidding when you said it was a disaster. I am so sorry. But it must've been cool to meet the Falcons," Marly remarked.

"Yeah, I guess so," I uttered.

"You guess? Any girl would kill to meet them and become close friends with them," she replied giddily.

"Well, that's not all I did."

"What do you mean?" she asked.

"I slept with Luke Nash the night that I had my blackout."

"No way, I can't believe this. You are so lucky," Marly said as her eyes lit up.

"No, I'm not. He's just like all the rest. He only wants one thing," I explained, walking back to my blanket.

"I could have a one-night stand with him and not care one bit," she smiled.

"That's you, I'm not like that. I want more from a guy than a roll in the hay."

From behind us, a voice called out, "Vicki! Hey Vicki, come over here for a minute!"

I sat up, looked around, and saw my brother in the parking lot standing next to a nice sports car. I stood up and started walking towards him until I saw that Luke was sitting in the car. I stopped dead in my tracks.

"Matt, please take your friend away from here. I don't wish to see him. You can stay, but he has to go!" I yelled to him.

Matt stepped up to me and said, "He just wants to talk with you for a few minutes."

"I have nothing to say to him."

"Come on, give him a break," Matt implored.

"Why did he send you over? Why couldn't he have come over here and tell me himself?" I inquired. Yelling in Luke's direction, I added, "What's the matter, too immature to talk me himself?"

"Just talk to him and stop acting stupid. You know if he gets out of the car he'll be mobbed," Matt remarked, taking me by the arm and leading me to the car. As we approached the car, Matt said, "Now, get in there. I'm not letting you out until you at least hear him out."

"All right, there's no need to be pushy," I said, opening the door and getting in. "Start talking, because I'm only giving you five minutes, and then I'm out of here," I told Luke.

"Why did you leave like that?" he asked.

"Because I wanted to, and I could," I sneered.

"I was going to bring you home in the morning."

"I felt it was better for both of us that I left the way I did," I explained. "How did you know where to find me?"

"Matt told me back in Maine where you guys lived."

"I'll be sure to thank him when I get out," I snickered.

"How can you say that it was the best thing to do? I was hurt and very worried about you," he expressed softly.

"Oh please, you don't care about me. You're just like any other rock musician; you're in love with yourself and make no room in your life for anyone else."

"I do care. I'm your friend, and I'm not like the others. It's just that I'm not ready for a commitment yet," he explained.

"Whatever, I have to go. I have a real friend waiting for me," I said, reaching for the door handle.

"Vicki, wait! I have something to tell you from my heart," he cried.

"Make it quick, please."

He just sat there and didn't say a word.

"I knew it; you can't do it. Well, it's been nice seeing you again," I jeered, as I got out of the car.

The next thing I knew, he drove the car in front of me and yelled for me to get back in. I turned around, started to walk away, then stopped when I heard a car door open and shut. The sound of footsteps grew louder and closer until I felt hands on my body lifting me up. It was Luke; he carried me over his shoulders and put me in the car.

"What are you doing, and where are you taking me?" I asked loudly.

"I don't know, somewhere secluded so we can be alone," he responded.

We were about halfway down the road when he turned off onto a dirt road. He parked the car off to the side near some bushes, then got out and came around to my side of the car to let me out.

"Well, now that you have found your secluded place, tell me what you want from me," I stated, turning the radio on.

"Please, turn it off, and just hear me out for once," Luke implored.

"Fine, but make it quick. I do still have a friend waiting back at the beach, and she's probably wondering what happened to me by now," I told him, shutting off the radio.

"I would like to sing a song that I wrote for you. It's called, 'The Fact Is.'"

A SUMMER AFFAIR

I nodded my head. We started walking hand in hand down a small path which led us to a bridge over a ravine. We stopped near an enormous rock; he lifted me up on it and then began singing to me. While he was singing, he danced around in front of me, then took a hold of my hand and gazed deeply into my eyes. Around the second verse, Luke gently picked me up off the rock, pulled me to him, and we began dancing very slowly. The way that he held me, looked at me, and sang to me made me feel like melting right there in his embrace.

"That was beautiful. The words reminded me of a poem about roses," I cried as he stopped singing.

"Please, don't cry," he pleaded.

"I can't help it; I was just so moved by the song."

"I am glad to hear you say that, and I hope that you now understand what I have been trying to tell you."

"Yes, I do. If you don't mind, I'd like to hear it again," I hinted.

Without another word spoken, he sang the song to me again. When he finished, he pulled me closer, then pressed his mouth against mine. The kiss didn't feel sexual; it felt like the kiss of love.

"No, please stop. We can't do this," I whined, pulling away from him.

"What is wrong? It was just a kiss."

"I don't want to get my hopes up and then be let down again."

"I don't want that to happen, either. Let's just take it one day and one step at a time," he proposed.

"Okay, we'll just go with the flow of things," I replied.

"We should probably get going. Matt and your friend are waiting for us," he suggested as we headed back to the car.

When we got back, Marly and Matt were waiting by my car. We got out of the car and stood in the shade by a tree so that nobody would see Luke.

"So, is everything okay with you two, and what are you doing tonight?" Marly asked me.

"Uh—" I started, but Luke interceded.

"Everything is fine, and we're leaving for New York tonight. We'll be there for a couple of days, if she doesn't mind," Luke told Marly.

"Yes! Oh, yes, I'll go!" I squealed.

"Great. I'll pick you up around four o'clock; that way we will get there by eight."

"Why by eight?" I questioned.

"Because we have dinner reservations at a little bistro I know about."

"When did you make the reservations?"

"Right after we arrived at the motel."

"How did you know things would work out this way?" I posed.

"You ask a lot of questions, but I happen to have a lot of answers. To answer your last question, I know you," he smiled as he got his car.

"Should I pack some clothes?" I asked, smiling.

"If you want to, you can. It doesn't matter," he grinned and drove away with Matt.

I brought Marly to her house, drove quickly to my house, ran in and up the stairs. Time must go by really fast when you're excited, because it was 4:00 p.m. when I finished painting my face. My mom called up to me and told me that Luke was downstairs waiting. Quickly, I grabbed my suitcase, put my black strapless mini-dress on, and snatched my heels and purse, then raced down the stairs. Luke stood up from his seat in awe as I approached him in the kitchen.

"Wow! You look stunning," he exclaimed.

"Thank you, but I hope that I am not over dressed."

"No, that dress is perfect," Luke smiled.

"Are we taking your car or mine?" I asked, sitting down on the chair with him.

"Neither, we're going by train, as long as it's okay with you."

"That's fine with me. I've never been on a train before," I smiled.

Luke picked up my suitcase and took it out to his car while I said goodbye to my mom and brother. When we finally arrived at the train station, it was about five o'clock, and the train had just pulled in. As soon as we boarded the train, we put our luggage away then headed for the dining car for some refreshments.

"Luke, just out of curiosity, what are we doing for transportation once we're in New York?" I asked.

"There will be a limo waiting for us at the station," he answered.

"I just have two more questions."

"Go ahead and ask away.".

"What part of New York are we going to? And where's the rest of the band?"

"We're going to New York City, and the band is in Brooklyn. We'll meet up with them the day after tomorrow," he replied.

By the time we arrived in New York City, we were felling well. The limo was long and white; inside of it there was a TV, VCR, phone, and a small liquor cabinet. It was my first time in a limo, as well as a train, and it was an awesome experience with both. The restaurant we were dining in was called Le Bistro. It was a cozy little restaurant on the corner Fifth Avenue and Main Street. Luke behaved like a perfect gentleman; he opened the door to the limo for me and then did the same at the restaurant.

The maitre d' seated us in a comfortable booth at the back of the dining room so we could have some privacy. He handed us our menus and stood quietly by our table while we glanced at our options. Everything looked scrumptious, but very expensive. Feeling out of place, I closed my menu and set it down.

"What's wrong?" Luke asked me, noticing my menu in front of me.

"Nothing, it's just that everything is so expensive. I don't want you to waste your money," I mumbled.

"Don't worry about it, you can order whatever you would like. Money is no object," he responded.

"Are you sure?"

"Positive," he smiled.

"Would the gentleman care to order a bottle of wine or champagne?" the maitre d' asked Luke.

"Yes, we would like a bottle of your best champagne," Luke told him.

"Splendid. I'll have your waiter bring it right out," the maitre d' replied, then turned and walked away.

When the waiter came with our champagne, Luke told him to leave the bottle in the bucket and said that we were ready to order. Luke ordered Veal Parmesan and a caesar salad, while I ordered Oysters Rockefeller and a chef's salad.

"Let's make a toast," Luke suggested as he lifted his glass.

"What are we toasting to?"

"We are toasting to the friendship that we have now and to a beautiful beginning."

"You are so sweet. Yes, to our friendship and a beautiful beginning," I smiled as we brought our glasses together.

Our meals arrived as we were setting our glasses down. After I took a small bite of the oysters, I realized that I didn't care for the taste of it. It turned out that Luke didn't like his dinner either, so we switched. For the rest of the time we were there, all we talked about was New York.

"Is there anything special that you would like to do next?" Luke asked me.

"I would like to go window shopping," I answered.

"Okay, I will get our coats and then we can leave," he smiled, stood up, and walked over to the cloakroom.

When he returned, he helped me with my coat, left a nice-size tip for the waiter, and we left. We decided to walk along

A SUMMER AFFAIR

Main Street where most of the good stores are. There were many nice things and I wished that I could have bought them all. The last shop we looked at was a small boutique. I wanted to take a quick look inside, so we went in. We were browsing around when I saw a beautiful white mink coat.

"Do you like it?" Luke asked.

"It's okay," I answered as we headed out the door.

"How would you like to take a carriage ride through Central Park?" he inquired.

"I would love to," I replied.

"Okay, you go ahead and get in, I'll be right back. I have to go back to the boutique because I left my sunglasses in there," he told me, walking away.

Luke came back, got in the carriage, and the driver proceeded down the street.

"Are you cold, Vicki?" Luke asked.

"A little bit," I nodded.

"Close your eyes and you'll get a nice surprise."

I happily closed my eyes and then I felt something soft and fluffy wrap around me. I opened my eyes and saw the mink coat that I had admired from the boutique.

"Oh. Luke. How—why—?" I was flabbergasted.

"I thought this might keep you warmer than the one you already have. Plus, I saw how much you liked it, so I bought it," he replied with a big smile.

"But, the price was a bit extravagant," I told him.

"It's okay; nothing is too expensive or too good for a special friend of mine."

"Thank you so much. I don't know how I can ever repay you for what you have done," I told Luke as tears began to form in my eyes.

"You're welcome. As long as you stay sweet, that will be payment enough."

I immediately turned to face him. I leaned over and kissed him on his cheek while quickly and gently squeezing him. It was such a romantic ride; the moon and stars were gleaming brightly, and the city lights seemed to follow us as if we were the moons and they were the stars.

"Are you enjoying the ride, Vicki?" Luke asked.

"Yes, it's wonderful. I will never forget any of this for as long as I live."

He smiled and kissed my hand.

We rode around Central Park for a while and then headed back to the limo. It was waiting in front of the Omni Biltmore Hotel, but we didn't get in. Instead, Luke brought me inside and checked us in.

"Luke, where's my suitcase?" I questioned.

"It's already in your room. The bellboy brought our luggage up to our rooms earlier while we were out," he answered.

We took the elevator up to our rooms. I had never been on a glass outdoor elevator, and it was amazing. We were very high before the elevator finally stopped. The view was breathtaking; we could almost see the entire city. Our rooms were on the twenty-fifth floor, and my room was right across the hall from Luke's. He walked me to my room and opened the door for me.

"Would you like to come in for a drink?" I asked him.

"Sure, but just for a few minutes," he answered, walking in the room with me.

"Why don't you fix us a drink while I change into something more comfortable?" I suggested.

As he began pouring us a couple of brandy shots, I went in the next room and slipped into one of my nightgowns. I decided to keep my coat on because it felt so nice and was so beautiful. I never wanted to take it off.

"I thought that you were going to change?" Luke inquired, noticing that I still had my coat on as I came back out of the other room.

"I did, it's just that I wanted to keep my coat on," I replied.

"Are you cold?" he asked, handing me my brandy.

"Thank you. No, I just love this coat, and I don't want to take it off," I responded, sitting on the loveseat and holding my coat closer to me.

"I'm glad that you like it so much, but you should take it off before something spills on it," he remarked.

"Your right, I'll take it off," I said, standing up to take it off.

"Here, allow me to help you with that," he suggested as he came up behind me and started to take it off. He took it off very slowly and gently, so it wouldn't get ruined. When it was just about off, he stopped and didn't say a word or move a muscle.

"Is there something wrong?" I inquired, turning to face him.

"No. I was just thinking about something, that's all," he answered as he walked over to the closet.

"What were you thinking about?" I asked.

"I need to go to my room for a second; I have to take my medicine."

"What kind of medicine?"

"It's a special prescription for my allergies," he responded as he walked out the door.

While I waited for him to return, I went in the bedroom and lay down on the bed. A few minutes later, I heard him come into the room. I pretended to be sleeping. He sat down next to me on the bed and covered me up with my coat.

"Vicki, I know that you can't hear me, but I still feel that I have to tell you this. Maybe you'll hear what I'm saying in your dreams. I care about you, and I don't want to hurt you. When I saw you standing there in your nightgown, all that I wanted to do was pick you up, carry you in here, and make love to you. I knew I couldn't treat you like that, though. That's why I feel we should stay away from each other for a while," he whispered, brushing my hair back with his fingers.

Then he lightly kissed my forehead, said goodbye and goodnight, and left. What he didn't realize was that I had heard everything that he had said. I needed to figure out a way to get him back to my room so that we could talk. Then it hit me! I could call his room and say I was scared. The telephone rang three times before he picked up.

"Hello," he said.

"Luke, please help me," I cried.

"What's wrong?" he asked.

"I thought I heard someone in the room with me."

"That was me."

"No, it couldn't have been, because I just heard it," I told him.

"Where did you hear the noise?"

"It was coming from the bathroom," I uttered.

"Okay, I'll be right over," he told me and then hung up.

He entered the room quietly, just in case there was an intruder. Luke checked the entire room, but he didn't find anyone or anything.

"If there was someone here, I probably scared them off," he remarked. "Are you all right?"

"I think so; I'm just a bit shaken up," I responded.

"It's all right, I'm here now, and I'm not leaving. You have nothing to worry about; I won't let anyone hurt you," he told me as he pulled me to him.

"Thanks, but how can you do that if you leave?"

"Who said anything about me leaving?" he asked.

"You did earlier," I cried as I ran in the bathroom.

"No, I didn't," he called out through the door.

"Yes, you did," I told him as I opened the door. "You told me that you felt that it was better if we didn't see each other for a while."

"What I meant was that I didn't want you falling head over heels for me," he explained, leading me into the living room.

"Don't worry, I won't," I assured him.

"I'll get my pillows and blankets from my room and stay here with you tonight," he replied, walking towards his room.

When he returned, we sat down on the bed together and watched television for a little while. Sometime later, Luke got up and went in the bathroom. As he was coming out, he started taking off his shirt, and that's when I realized how really well built he was.

"I never noticed it before, but you have the cutest little feet," I giggled, looking down at his feet.

"Why, thank you," he remarked.

He put his pillow and blankets on the floor next to the side of the bed where I would be sleeping. We kissed each other on the cheek, and said goodnight.

"Before I go to sleep, I want to thank you for everything that you have been doing for me," I said.

"Your welcome, I will always be here for you," he smiled and reached for my hand. We held hands as I drifted off to sleep.

- 9 -
Choices/Farewell

I woke up the next morning and noticed Luke had already woken up and gotten out of bed. I looked around in each of the rooms, but there was no sign of him. I called the front desk to see if they knew where he might be, but they didn't. I jumped in the shower, got dressed, then did my hair and face. This day was definitely not starting out well. *How could he leave like that?* I thought to myself. By the time I had left the hotel, it was lunchtime, which meant busy streets. The limo that Luke had gotten for us was waiting outside the hotel. I got in and asked the driver to drive around for a while.

We went by a little shop that looked nice, so I asked him to drop me off, and then come back in thirty minutes. I browsed around for a while when an outfit on a rack caught my eye. It was a two-piece outfit, a leather v-neck blazer and a mini skirt. The clerk told me that I could try it on in the dressing room at the back of the shop. I picked up the outfit, went over to the dressing room, and tried it on. It fit me perfectly, and it looked good on me. I never thought that black leather would look right on me, but I was wrong. The outfit was missing a few things though: a pair of shoes, a sterling silver chain necklace and matching earrings. After I changed back into my street clothes, I went to look for the missing items. As I turned to go back to the dressing room, I saw Luke standing there.

"What are you doing here?" I asked.

"Watching you dress and undress," he smiled.

"How long have you been watching me?" I questioned.

"From the time you walked into the store," Luke answered.

"Why didn't you say anything to me or approach me? Why did you leave like that this morning?" I inquired, walking out of the dressing room.

"Vicki, wait up," he called out to me as I kept walking away from him.

"Why should I?"

"Because I want to explain why I left this morning," he replied as he caught up to me.

"Thank you, Miss," The clerk said to me at the counter as I paid for my stuff.

"You're welcome. Have a nice day," I told her and then walked outside.

"All right, so explain why you left the way you did," I said, stopping at the store window.

"I forgot that I had a meeting with my manager this morning."

"Couldn't you have left me a note or something?"

"I didn't have time; I overslept. Plus, I thought I would've been back before you woke up," he explained.

"You could've left a message with the front desk on your way out," I told him.

"You're right, I am sorry for not thinking about your feelings. I hope that you can forgive me," Luke expressed.

"I guess that I have to forgive you, because I'm not your lady. We have no commitment or anything, so there's no reason for me to be this mad," I told him, walking towards the limo.

He opened the door for me, helped me into the limo, and lightly kissed my hand. Then he said, "You are my lady."

"What do you mean by that?" I asked as he got in the limo.

"You are the only woman I have ever met who I have such string feelings for. No other woman has ever made me feel the way you do," Luke revealed to me.

"That is very nice to know," I said, looking away from him to hide the enormous smile that formed across my face.

Then I noticed the limo coming to a stop, so I turned to Luke, and asked, "Why are we stopping?"

"I need to get the key to the studio from my manager; I forgot it when I was here earlier," he responded.

"Isn't he going to be there tomorrow? Why don't you have your own key?"

"No, and that's just the way the manager wants it. I'll be right back," he replied, getting out of the limo.

I wanted to watch where he went so I could see what his manager looked like, but I couldn't bring myself to do it. It would be an invasion of his privacy. I hated feeling as if I couldn't trust him. A few minutes had passed and the curiosity was eating away at me inside; I had to look and see. When I did look up, I wished that I hadn't. He came out of the building with a tall, voluptuous blonde on his arm. He turned to her and kissed her. From where I was, it didn't appear to be a friendly kiss. Their lips seemed locked longer than a normal and friendly kiss. Boy was I ever jealous and hurt, but I knew that he was not mine. I think that's what hurt the most.

Luke got back in the limo. I asked him about the key, and he said he got it. After that, we didn't speak to each other for just about the whole ride. When I finally did say something to him, it had nothing to do with what had happened between him and the mysterious blonde.

"What are we doing tonight?" I asked him.

"I thought that we would go to this nightclub on the east side," he answered.

"I was under the impression that you didn't like disco or pop music," I said.

"I don't; this one plays only rock-n-roll music. Besides, their drinks are dirt cheap," he replied.

I thought to myself that this would be the perfect place to find out how he truly feels about me and to see if he's the jealous type. We went back to the hotel to change into different attire. I decided to wear the outfit that I had just purchased, and Luke wore black jeans, a jade-green silk shirt, and black cowboy boots. The boots that I had on were like his, except mine had tassels on the sides. When we arrived at the nightclub, I was very surprised to see that it was jam-packed with people so early in the evening. Usually at 9:30 p.m. there is hardly anyone in a bar; but then again, this was New York City.

"Wow! This place is hopping!" I shouted to Luke; the music was blaring, and I wanted to make sure that he could hear me.

"It's always like this," he stated.

"Let's go find a couple of seats, if we can," I told him.

"Okay, we'll get our drinks from the waitress once we sit down," he replied.

We found a table and two chairs on the second level near the dance floor. I peered through the crowd to see the types of people in attendance. It seemed like there were more guys than girls, which would work out great for my plan to test Luke and make him jealous.

"Do you want to shoot some pool?" Luke asked me.

"Sure, but only one game. I'm not really very good at it, so I don't want to embarrass myself too much."

We stood up, walked back downstairs and over to the poolroom. On our way, I spotted a guy that would be perfect for my plan. He was about my height, not too tall, not too short; he had long chocolate-colored hair, big brown eyes, and was slender. The more I looked at him, the more familiar he became. I knew that I had seen him before, but I just couldn't place where and when.

I strutted past him and turned my head to see if he was looking. He was. While Luke was setting up the pool table, I tried to figure out a way to get the guy's attention again. When I turned to look for him, I couldn't find him. I walked over to the front of the table, picked up my cue and started the game with my first scratch.

"What a goofball, I can't believe that got a scratch," I chuckled.

"It's okay; we all make mistakes," Luke said while taking his first shot. He got three balls in, and then said, "I'll be right back. I have to go use the little boys' room."

I watched him as he walked away; he was so sexy and handsome. Just as I was getting into position to shoot my next ball, I backed right into someone.

"Oops! I am truly sorry," I exclaimed as I turned to see who I had hit. It turned out to be the guy I saw earlier.

"No problem. Haven't I seen you somewhere before?" the stranger asked me.

"Only, if you've been in Rhode Island or Maine," I responded.

"Yeah, that's it. I live in Providence, so I'm sure I must have seen you at a concert or something," he replied.

"Wow! This is so cool. I never thought I would be meeting up with someone from my neck of the woods here tonight," I replied gleefully.

"Yeah, who would've thought?" he said.

"By the way, my name is Vicki," I told him, extending out my hand to him.

"Hi, my name is Bobby Vister," he smiled.

We began talking about his life, my life, how I met and became friends with the Falcons. His eyes lit up when I mentioned that I was there with Luke.

"Do you think that you could introduce me to him when he gets back?" Bobby asked.

"Sure, as long as you will show me how to hold my cue stick correctly," I replied.

"You have a deal."

I stood next to the side of the table, he came up behind me, and put his hands over mine. He started showing me how to hold it, aim it, and shoot it. We were giggling so much about my little errors that I didn't notice that Luke had returned until I just happened to be looking up. He didn't look the least bit jealous or upset; I couldn't believe it. Maybe he didn't care after all. I still thought that he did after the song for me, bought the fur coat, and took me on this trip to New York City. I figured I would try a couple of more maneuvers, and if they didn't work, I'd just give up.

The next thing I did was drink two shots of tequila. Then I took Bobby's hand and led him to the dance floor. The more we danced, the tipsier I became. Luke didn't seem effected by our close dancing, or the fact that I was gazing into Bobby's eyes. He just stood there by the dance floor and watched us with a smile. A few minutes later, Luke came up to us on the dance floor and told me that it was my turn to shoot. Bobby and I stopped dancing and walked back to the poolroom where Luke was waiting patiently.

"All right, four in the corner pocket," I called out, pointing to where I was going to shoot the ball.

Carefully, I aimed the cue, put my fingers in position, shot, and the ball went right in the pocket. I started jumping up and down and screaming. I couldn't believe that I had made the shot. Now all I had to do to win was get the eight ball in the pocket that I called out.

"Now, arch your back, stand at an angle, aim, and shoot," Bobby explained as he put his hands on my waist to help maneuver my body.

I looked over at Luke to see if he was upset, but he wasn't. I just shrugged my shoulders, looked back at the eight ball, and shot it into the side pocket.

"I won! I can't believe it!" I shrieked. "Let's all celebrate. I'm going to buy us a bottle of wine."

When I came back from the bar with the wine, Luke and Bobby weren't in the poolroom. I looked around the crowd and spotted them sitting at our table. They were talking and laughing away about something. I think it had to do with me, because when I approached the table, they stopped immediately.

"We were just talking about you," Luke smiled as I sat down next to him.

"Is that so? All good things, I hope," I chuckled.

"Of course, I can't see anything bad on you or about you," Bobby smiled, looking me over.

"Why, thank you. I'll take that as a compliment. Hey, let's not waste any of this wine, drink up."

After two bottles, we were all feeling good. We laughed, sang, talked, laughed some more, and sang some more.

"Vicki, I'm going to go to the store. I'll be right back," Luke told me.

"What are you getting at the store?" I asked him.

"Some gum," he answered.

"Oh, okay," I said.

"Will you be okay while I'm gone?"

"I'll be fine; I have Bobby here to keep me company," I replied as I smiled over at Bobby.

"All right, then. I shall return," Luke said and walked away.

We continued drinking while Luke was gone. I apologized for not formally introducing him to Luke, and he said not to worry about it. A little while later, I went over to the bar to talk with the manager about Luke.

"Excuse me, sir, but do you think that my friend could go on stage and sing a couple of songs?" I asked him.

"Who's your friend?" he inquired.

"Luke Nash, he's the lead singer of the Falcons," I answered,

"Of course, he sings in here every time he's in town," he smiled widely.

He seemed to be a gentleman; his face appeared to be soft, and he had short blond hair and blue eyes. His body seemed like a fortress, with muscles bulging everywhere I looked. Bobby came up to us and joined in on our conversation about Luke. Just then, Luke showed up.

"You were gone for a while; I was beginning to get worried," I cried softly as I embraced him.

"I'm okay, sorry if I worried you. Troy, give me a gin and tonic. Actually, make it a double," Luke remarked.

"Luke, the manager said that you could get up on stage and sing a couple of songs if you wanted to. That is, if you're up to it," I told him.

"I'm fine. I'll go right now. I'll talk to you afterwards," he smiled, putting his glass down on the counter.

"Okay, I'll be right in front cheering for you," I smiled.

The way he just walked away from me made me forget about my plan to make him jealous. *Why was acting like this?* I thought. Bobby noticed the look of concern on my face, so he gently squeezed my hand and led me to the front of the stage. Everything seemed to be getting better; Luke would glance over at me in the crowd and smile while he was singing.

When he was finished with the first song, he came off stage, strutted over to a tall blonde woman, and proceeded to bring her on stage with him. Then to top it all off, he started singing the song that he not only sang to me, but that he presumably had written for me. She was hardly wearing anything, and he was all over her. Breathing and kissing her on the neck, Luke didn't notice me waving to him. Crushed, I turned to Bobby and asked him if he could bring me back to the hotel.

Before we left, I took off my fur coat, walked up to the stage, and threw it at Luke. Then I yelled to him, "It's over. You can give your bimbo friend the garbage that you bought me, because I don't want it."

"Are you going to be okay?" Bobby asked me as we walked out of the bar.

"Yeah, I guess so. It's just that he said that he wrote that song for me, and that I was his lady."

"I thought that you two were only friends."

"We are, but we have shared things that can only compare with lovers."

"I understand. Maybe when you get back to Rhode Island, we can get together sometime," Bobby suggested as we neared the hotel.

"Sure, I'd like that. I'm in the phonebook, so look me up sometime," I told him.

"Okay, see you around," he replied.

"See ya, and thanks for everything," I smiled, kissing him on the cheek.

When I walked by Luke's room, I didn't hear anything, so I figured that he hadn't returned yet. I walked into my room, undressed, and hopped in the shower. After I cleansed and rinsed my whole body, I turned the water off and got out. As I was putting my nightgown on, I felt a pair of hands go over my eyes.

"Guess who?" the stranger asked.

"Luke, what are you doing here?" I questioned after I realized who it was.

"I had to see you and feel you. I can't control myself any longer," he responded as he wrapped his arms around me.

"You don't even know what you're talking about. You're drunk," I said, pushing him away.

"I'm not drunk, and I do know what I am saying. Just to prove it to you, I will take a shower and drink some black coffee," he remarked, walking towards the telephone in the other room.

"Yes, I would like to order some coffee for room 211," Luke said to a clerk on the other end of the line.

He hung up the telephone, went back into the bathroom, turned on the shower, and got in. While he was in the bathroom, I went out on the patio to think. *Should I give him a chance to explain or what?* I thought to myself. *He is the man I had fantasies of for half of my life. He was there when I needed him, and we were friends at one time. I guess I owe him that much.*

As I was coming off the patio, room service came with coffee. I took my cup and went back out on the balcony to do some more thinking.

I just don't understand him, why does he keep playing these games with me? Maybe he's doing all of this because of the accident. He did say that he was going to make it up to me for as long as he lived, but I can't live like this. I have to tell him that I meant what I said back at the bar. Especially after his behavior back at the bar and when he presumably went to get the key from his manager.

"He told me that he wrote that song for me. How could he sing it to that bimbo?" I said to myself.

"That song was written for you," Luke replied from behind me.

I jerked my head, jumped, and my body quivered from the shock of hearing his voice.

"How can you really expect me to believe you after everything that has happened?" I questioned, turning my back to him.

"Like what?" he inquired.

"Like when you told me how you felt at the rock, then you turn around and lie to me about your manager and the key," I sneered.

"What did I supposedly lie about?"

"You told me that you were getting the key from your manager, but when you came out, you were kissing some blonde. Then there was the incident at the bar with my song and that blonde bombshell!" I yelled.

"There's no need to be so loud. You're going to get us kicked out of here. Now let me try to explain myself. First of all, I was drunk and confused about the way I am around women, and when I'm around you," Luke explained.

"You know what? I shouldn't even care about any of this. You're only treating me the way you are because you are trying to make up for the accident that you caused in Maine.

I'm not your girlfriend or your wife, anyway. Heck, I don't even know if I want to be your friend, because friends don't lie to each other," I expressed sadly.

"I am not doing all of this to make up for what I did to you," he replied.

"Then why? I do have a right to know," I cried.

He didn't say anything. I couldn't believe it. Why was he doing this to me?

"I was right; you don't care about me at all," I said to him, walking right past him.

As he grabbed a hold of my arm, he replied, "I do care about you. You just don't understand."

"Then tell me what it is I don't understand," I told him.

"I don't know—" Luke started to say.

"Don't know what?"

Again he was speechless; it hurt so badly inside that I began to cry.

"Vicki, please don't cry," he pleaded.

"Why? It doesn't bother you one bit that I'm hurting. I wish I wasn't behaving like this in front of you," I wept softly.

"Why do you say that?"

"You have been a fantasy of mine for half of my life. I have loved you for so long," I responded, weeping.

"Do you really feel that way?" he asked, surprised.

"I did, but I have faced reality. We were just friends, nothing more," I answered.

There was a sort of stillness between us for about five minutes. Neither one of us looked at each other during that time.

"Well, there it is. It's been fun and everything, Mr. Nash. I've really enjoyed the times that we have spent together, but now it's time to say farewell."

"What is this 'Mr. Nash' bologna? Why this sudden change in your attitude?" he inquired. "I thought we were friends."

"We can't be friends like we have been. That's why I have to treat you like the person you are. Can't you see how much

I love you and how it kills me to be around you and not have you?" I replied, starting to cry again.

"Vicki, please just listen to me," he implored.

"No, just go," I told him as I walked back into the other room.

"Vicki, please just hear me out," he begged.

"No! I told you to leave."

He threw up his hands, walked out of my room, and I went back to the balcony. I couldn't take this pain anymore. It was too unbearable; I wanted to end it all. I walked out onto the ledge and just stood there for a few moments. The next thing I knew, there were sirens below me. They were coming from about five different fire engines. There were people banging on my door. Not wanting to cause any more harm or trouble, I decided to stop what I was doing, pack up my things, and leave. After I gathered my things, I left my room, got on the elevator, and headed downstairs. As I was getting off the elevator, I saw Luke running up to me.

"Vicki, why are you leaving?" he asked, walking up to me.

"I can't stay here any longer. The longer I stay, the more harm it will cause everyone. I have already caused an alarm in the hotel, so before I embarrass you any further, I'm going back to Rhode Island."

"You haven't and you're not embarrassing me. Nobody even knows it was you up on the ledge," he told me.

"You knew that it was me, so you can't be certain that everyone else doesn't know. Goodbye, Mr. Nash," I remarked, looking around at the people standing around watching us.

"Stop with the 'Mr. Nash' malarkey. If you had let me explain myself earlier, none of this would've happened," he said.

"I did give you a chance, but you wouldn't say anything."

"You're right. It's just hard for me to say. I know that's no excuse, and I take full responsibility for what has happened. Haven't you figured out, yet, what I have been trying to tell you?" he asked.

"No, I haven't. In fact, I don't want to know. It's only going to be more head games, and I don't need it," I snapped.

"No, it won't. I promise."

"Please, spare me your empty words," I retorted, walking towards the front door. Unfortunately, I couldn't get out because crowds of people were blocking my way.

"Just listen to him, lady," a tall man in a dark suit said to me.

Then everyone else began shouting the same thing, and making sure that I wasn't leaving until I heard him out.

"All right, I might as well listen. You people won't let me to leave until I do," I said, walking back towards Luke.

"I'm glad to see that you are willing to give me a chance," he smiled.

"I didn't have much of a choice, thanks to your fan club. So, just start talking," I told him.

"I won't waste precious time on your remark when I have something more important to say," he replied.

"Good," I sneered.

"First, the song that I wrote for you was my way of expressing how I feel inside," he uttered.

"Don't tell me that you're trying to say that you love me," I snickered loudly.

"Please, don't make fun of me. And yes, I do love you."

"Sorry," I replied.

"Don't you see that's why I arranged this trip? I wanted to finally tell you how I feel about you," he cried.

"Spare me your lies. I don't need them," I snarled.

"I'm not lying."

"Whatever you say. You don't even know the first thing about loving someone."

"You're right, I don't. But I'm sure if we both tried hard enough to love each other, it would work. You could show me how to love you the way you deserve," he responded, reaching for my hand.

"How do I know you're telling me the truth?"

"This is how," he answered, reaching his other hand into his pocket, pulling out a little black box.

"What's this?" I inquired.

"I want the whole world to know how much I love this lady!" Luke shouted to the crowd. "I want everyone to hear me ask this beautiful lady to be by my side forever!"

I just stood there in amazement, as did everyone else in the lobby. My mouth was hanging open, tears filled my eyes, and my hands were shaking. "Do you really mean it?" I asked him.

"Yes, if I have to, I will get down on my hands and knees and beg," he remarked as he started to get in the position.

He took my hand in his, slipped a large diamond ring on my finger, and kissed my hand.

"I know that it will be difficult at times, especially with both of us living in different parts of the country. But I'm willing to try if you are," Luke expressed.

"I don't know," I said.

"I love you, Vicki. You've made me see and feel things that I never knew I had or knew existed," he explained.

"I understand, it's just—"

"Will you please marry me and be with me for the rest of our lives?"

"Yes, I will marry you!" I cried.

At that moment, the whole lobby began clapping, whistling, and cheering. Then Luke let out a big scream, picked me up, and swung me around in his arms. The excitement brought out laughter and tears from inside of me. Hand in hand, we walked back upstairs, but this time, we went into his room. Luke thought that we might need to talk some more, but with more privacy.

"Are you sure that you're ready to give up life in the fast lane?" I asked him, sitting down on the sofa.

"Yes, but I will need your love and guidance to help me. Plus, I know that the band will also help me, and we will be seeing each other more, now," he replied, sitting down next to me.

"How are we ever going to manage this?" I questioned.

"My tour ends next spring; you'll be out of college sometime after that. After that we can move away together and get a house of our own," Luke explained.

"I don't want to start college in one place for a year and then transfer the next. It's just too much of a hassle, but I guess it's a small price to pay for happiness," I sighed. "But what about from now until then?"

"I will have two weekends off each month, and in between those times, you can come visit me while I'm on the road."

"That sounds good, as long as I have the money to do that. This means that I will have to get a job for sure. But, then again, if I get a job, I can't be taking too much time off," I replied.

"Don't worry about the money; I will pay for it all. So, now you don't need a job, because I will give you money whenever you need or want it," he told me.

"I can't believe this; it's like a dream come true," I cried.

"That's what I am here for," he smiled. "Can you wait until next year to have me around all of the time?"

"Oh, yes. It will be worth the wait. Any time I feel lonely or sad, all I have to do is look at this ring," I smiled as I gazed down at my ring.

"There's an inscription on the inside," he remarked.

I took it off, looked on the inner part, and read it aloud, "*Our love will be forever.* It's beautiful, thank you so much," I wept.

"Just like the beauty who is wearing it," he replied, slipping it back on my finger.

Then he stood up, walked over to the stereo, put a cassette in it, and came back to the sofa. He extended his hand out to me. I took it and he helped me up. The song wed danced to was called, "Eternity." As we were dancing, Luke stared into my eyes and began singing along with the song. Then he lowered me back and started gently kissing my neck. His hands slowly moved up my back, as he lifted me back up. The next song to come on was called, "No More Farewells."

Luke picked me up and carried me over to the bedroom where he laid me down. After an intense and passionate hour of kissing, he undressed me, then himself. Next, he gradually slid his warm body on top of mine and began fondling my lower body with his.

It was so beautiful and wonderful; it didn't even feel like sex. I had never had an experience like this with any other man. I felt like we were flying on a cloud, or soaring through the skies like birds. We went on for what seemed like days, but it was actually a few hours. Tired from the love making, we stopped, snuggled up to one another, and fell asleep.

The next morning, we rushed around both of our rooms, packing, showering, and getting dressed. Then after we checked out, Luke took me in the limo to the train station because I had to get back Rhode Island and he had to catch up with the band.

"I don't want to leave you, Luke," I cried.

"I know, and I don't want you to either. This is the way it has to be for now. It's only temporary," he replied, pulling me closer.

"I don't have to start college this year. I can wait until after your tour is over," I told him.

"No, I can't let you put your life on hold for me. Don't worry; we'll be seeing each other in a couple of weeks," Luke replied as we neared the train that I was taking.

"Do you promise?" I asked.

"Promise," he responded, putting his hand over his heart.

"I am sorry we didn't get a chance to hang out with the band and everything," I uttered.

"That's okay. I understand, and I'm sure that they will, too."

"I just don't know if I will make it without you," I sighed.

"I know that you will, because I am going to call you and write you as much as possible," he told me.

We embraced one another, and then kissed as if it were the last time we would ever see each other. Just as we pulled away from each other, the train's master yelled, "All aboard!"

Luke carried my suitcases on the train for me, and then held me in his arms as if he was afraid to let me go.

"I love you, Vicki," he cried.

"I love you, too."

"Just remember that you will always be my one and only lady," he expressed.

We said goodbye as I walked towards a window seat in the lounge, and he got off the train. As the train was pulling away from the station, I could see Luke waving back at me. Tears began streaming down my face as his body started to fade away from my sight. I had one last thought cross my mind as the train entered a dark tunnel. *My summer affair might be over, but my life is just beginning.*

Printed in the United States
33793LVS00002B/335